**Innoc**
(In

.... Scott

Published by Impresst Publishing

Copyright 2017 Ada Scott

Discover other titles by Ada Scott
at **www.adascott.com**

## Table of Contents

# Innocence For Sale #1

# Chapter 1

# Amy

# February 14th 2017

I could see my hand shaking as I cut the bread. Anybody watching might have thought I had a mild sandwich-phobia, but I had bigger things on my mind. Tonight was *the* night.

Anthony was picking me up at six, taking me out for dinner, and then he thought he was dropping me off at home again, but I had a surprise for him. My mom's friend, Agnes, was taking her out for a wild night of bingo and I'd been told not to wait up for them. Agnes was a bundle of energy for a retiree, and I was going to take the window of opportunity she'd given me to invite Anthony inside after dinner. To my room.

We'd been dating for a couple years. He'd asked me out shortly after I started at my new school. I'd been reluctant, of course; after all, it was a relationship disaster that forced me to change schools in the first place.

Not only that but, to look at him, any reasonable person would have classified Anthony as your stereotypical jock. *That* type was only interested in one thing and, traumatized as I was, I was *this close* to swearing off sex for life before I'd even gone all the way.

There was no way I could ever envision letting somebody get that close to me again... but he was so sweet. I was flattered. I was swept up by hope. It didn't hurt that he was easy on the eye.

So I said yes. I figured if he couldn't be patient, if he wasn't as nice to me when it sunk in that I was as far from putting out on the first date as any girl could be, I could just break it off. No harm, no foul, right?

Well, two years later, he was still waiting, and he was still being patient with me. I knew he *wanted* to go all the way. I'd said "no, not tonight" at least a thousand times when his hands wandered as we made out in his car.

It wasn't that I didn't like him, I did, but did I *love* him? Was that what I felt? I was so confused. It was a scary thing I was going to do tonight, but how much of my fear came from perfectly natural nerves, and how much from what happened with my last boyfriend?

Through the window I saw my mom rolling her chair slowly back to the house with a pile of mail on her lap. The driveway was really too rough for it, so the simple act of collecting the post was quite a workout.

If I was hired for any of the jobs I'd applied for, allowing me to graduate from waitress to something that paid a little better, I'd get her an electric wheelchair as soon as I could. She was getting to an age when she really needed it. Not only that, but damn it, she *deserved* something that would make life a little easier.

The screen door protested weakly as she rammed it open, followed by a few metallic scrapes and finally the creak of the hinges and hiss of the gas spring as it closed behind her. I didn't say anything about the ominous red stamp on the top letter on her lap. They were more the rule rather than the exception these days.

"Lunch is ready," I said.

My mom washed her hands and returned with the post still on her lap, before setting the pile on the table next to her plate. There was time for food before she went through the ordeal of how to juggle the bills.

We talked about anything *except* that while enjoying our treat. Ham and cheese between slices of bread may not have seemed like much of a treat to a lot of people, but it was for us. The Wilson family gave us a leg of ham from a pig they killed and smoked themselves. Mr. Bradley's current hobby was cheese-making, and he was giving it away all around the area just to show off. The bread was made from flour ground from the wheat on our own farm.

I was relieved that my voice wasn't shaking as badly as my hands. If it was, then my mom may not have been distracted enough by that pile of mail, looming over us like a warden on death row supervising a final meal. As things stood, I was able to keep my nerves under the radar.

While I was washing up, the look on her face made my heart sink as she opened each envelope. Eventually, one seemed to push her too far and I saw a tear fall down one cheek.

"Hey... hey Mom... cheer up, it might not happen."

Her quivering lip made me instantly regret saying such a ham-fisted nothing-cliché. I reached for the dishtowel so I could dry my hands and give her a hug.

"It *is* happening," she said.

"What is?"

The way her shoulders shook under my hands drove out all thoughts of my plans for this evening. I knelt by her chair, trying to comfort her.

"The bank is going to foreclose on us. No more extensions, no more deferred payments, no more anything."

She struggled to get each word out and they sounded like nails in a coffin. I could feel the color draining from my face as it sunk in. We were losing our home.

"It's my fault," she said through clenched teeth, more tears streaming down now.

"No, Mom…"

"It's *my* fault! It was all on me and… I wasn't enough."

"When? When is it happening?"

"June." She dropped the paper on the table and slumped in her chair.

"June! That's plenty of time! We'll think of something."

I tried to put every ounce of fictional optimism into my voice that I could muster. She wasn't buying it.

"They want it repaid in full."

"In *full*? How can they do that? It wasn't supposed to be paid off for, what? Another twelve years? Can't we just catch up to where we're supposed to be?"

"No more anything," she repeated quietly.

I held her tighter and rested my head on her shoulder, adding my own tears to the mix. The floor creaked under me and my heart clenched.

We *couldn't* be losing this house, this land. Dad walked on these floors. How could they take it away?

# Chapter 2

# Kris

# March 2017

"He's fucking crazy," said Daniel.

I tore my eyes away from Kevin and glanced in Daniel's direction. I almost managed to stifle a laugh. Almost. The handprint on his cheek from that apocalyptic slap he'd received was visible even in the club's dim and dynamic lighting.

Here I was thinking I had the wager in the bag, but if Kevin pulled this off, I'd consider it a thousand dollars well-spent. My potentially misplaced confidence came from the fact that the hostesses you get when you pay for bottle service are *specifically* forbidden to do anything beyond flirting with their customers. So when I had Lacey lay herself down on our table, that cute little skirt riding up to show off her panties while I did a body shot off her, I didn't think I could be outdone.

A thousand dollars for the most outrageous body shot of the night? Sure, it's spare change, but you couldn't deny it added some excitement to the evening, some thrill of competition.

Oh, and a shitload of humor too. Holy fuck, I laughed so hard that I thought I'd done some serious internal damage.

Shortly after I set the bar at what I thought was an impossibly high level, every eye in the room was drawn to some girl who'd just arrived. She was Cindy Johannson, a model who got her big break on one of those reality TV shows and was now really starting to take the world by storm.

That's who Daniel decided to try to get a body shot from. Well, she wound up a haymaker you could see coming from a mile away and slapped him so hard that you could hear it over the music. Daniel's head spun almost full circle while Kevin and I collapsed in hysterical laughter in our booth.

Somehow Daniel managed to negotiate his way out of an ass-kicking from all the white knights trying to impress Cindy, and came back to nurse his wounds. When I laid out the terms of the bet this evening, I was never worried about him as a threat anyway.

Truth be told, he was kind of an asshole. A harmless asshole, but annoying nonetheless. Somehow he managed to hang around, latch on to any ideas I had, and reap the rewards.

The only reason I knew him was because he worked at the same startup I did all those years ago, the kind of job where you get paid in stock options instead of actual money. Back then, twenty of us slept in one house while we prayed for our stock to be worth something.

Things like that are the kind of experiences that often result in lifelong friendships and business associations, but I'd never seen Daniel come up with an original concept of his own. I'd outgrown him, but he was a relic of my past that wouldn't seem to go away.

It was because of that past that I didn't tell him outright to fuck off. That and these occasional moments of comedy gold that he afforded me.

"Just watch him," I said and turned back to Kevin, who looked like he was getting ready to seal the deal. It was a good excuse to not have to make any more conversation with Daniel.

Kevin couldn't have been more different from Daniel. I didn't meet him until I was looking for partners and investors in my own first startup. He had the right background in coding that I needed, with a natural talent for entrepreneurship, plus he had the cash to buy into my idea. It was a perfect match.

Between the two of us, plus Daniel as a minority shareholder purely by virtue of being there when I came up with the idea and being willing to stump up some money, we built our company from zero to a multi-million dollar valuation. Three years later, when we sold it, we made a killing.

The waitress carried a tray with everything you need for a body shot in the direction of Kevin and Cindy. The pretty young model who had nearly knocked Daniel out looked appropriately scandalized when the shotglass, the salt and lemon were set down on the table. Kevin leaned over to whisper in her ear, and even from this distance I could tell she was faking it to keep up appearances.

The protest would be over qui... there! She nodded and rolled her eyes with a boys-will-be-boys smile.

"No *fucking* way!" said Daniel.

He could deny it all he wanted, but Cindy, the high-class supermodel, had just licked her own chest and was pouring salt on it. She took a deep breath, then put a wedge of lemon in her mouth and tilted her head to wait. The ball was in Kevin's court.

He leaned in, and whispered in Cindy's ear again. Her eyes went wide, but at least she didn't slap him when he cupped her salted breast and squeezed it hard enough that her firm flesh swelled at the top, while he made sure not a single grain of salt was left behind.

Never in my life had I seen a body shot take so long. I couldn't tell from here, but I wouldn't have been surprised if his tongue had slipped inside her top to find her nipple. He was practically sucking her tit right there in front of everybody.

Finally, when he couldn't handle the intense saltiness any longer, he downed his shot and locked lips with her around the lemon wedge, pushing her back on the bench seat with the force of his, let's call a spade a spade, kiss.

When they straightened themselves out again, Kevin pulled the lemon rind from his mouth in what could only be described as triumph. The well-groomed model looked like she'd just been fucked, judging by her panting and the way she was fanning herself. Even her perfect hair looked a little mussed up.

"Son of a bitch. Hey, you got like, a spare couple hundred? I'm a little short."

I turned back to our own table and picked up my beer, looking sideways at Daniel. "What the fuck do you mean you're short? Why get in on the bet if you couldn't afford to lose?"

"Hey, chill out. You know I'm good for it, I just don't carry that kind of cash around for no reason."

I rolled my eyes when he said he was good for it. That was contrary to previous experience. Still, it wasn't my problem.

"No deal, you can check with Kevin when he gets back and see if you can owe him. I don't think even *I* can spin this one into a win for me."

"Alright. Oh, speaking of wins, there's some rumors going around the office that you're considering a few offers on the business. Is that right?"

My eyes narrowed. "It *may* be right."

"Well, as one of the partners, I want to be kept informed of this kind of thing."

I bit my tongue for a second, willing my blood back from boiling point. The way his sense of entitlement crept into the tone of his voice set my teeth on edge like few other things. The nuisance of having him around was fast starting to outweigh the history we had.

"I've known you a long time now, but you're an employee with shares. Kevin and I are the founders and we'll let you *all* know when we have anything relevant to tell you."

Daniel, the 'partner' who wanted to be kept informed looked like he was ready to argue the point. I wondered if he'd like to be *closely* informed about his face hitting the table at top speed.

Thankfully, Kevin came back. He smothered the beginnings of an argument with a king's ransom worth of swagger. He slid into his seat and leaned back with his fingers interlaced behind his head.

I started the negotiations. "So, I think your effort fell a little short. I mean, I actually drank the tequila out of Lacey's belly button..."

"Fuck off," said Kevin.

He had a point. I sighed and pulled out my wallet to count out a thousand bucks. Daniel did the same. Well, almost the same, I supposed.

Kevin fanned himself with about seventeen hundred dollars before putting most of it away, leaving a couple notes out to wave at Lacey with. The hostess took an order for another round, with a special twinkle in her eye for me.

"What are you going to do with your ill-gotten gains?" I asked.

"I'm going to order a giant cake in the shape of a cock and balls to be delivered to your office."

"How much cock and balls cake can you get for a couple grand?" I asked.

"We're talking a few hundred pounds of cock and balls cake," said Kevin.

"You knew the answer to that suspiciously quickly," I said.

We all laughed, and the tension melted away as swiftly as it had built. Daniel asked Kevin how he'd managed to break the ice and Kevin told us all about it.

The music thumped and I surveyed the girls on the dancefloor who moved along with it. It was a good time to be alive and at the top of my game, but the same old girls around here were starting to bore me.

Lacey brought our drinks and slipped me her phone number on an otherwise blank card. She'd be good for a little fun later on, but nothing more.

Kevin checked the time and made an expression as if it was getting late. He tapped my arm with the back of his hand.

"Hey, you want a chance to redeem yourself?" he asked.

"In what way?"

"I've got a wager that I think only *you* would be crazy enough to accept. None of this under-the-sofa-cushions-money bullshit. Let's make it *really* interesting."

It had been a while since anybody had come up with a truly exciting challenge for me. Kevin knew better than anybody how far I'd go to win a bet, tonight being one of the rare occasions when the money had flowed in his direction. Something in his voice piqued my interest though.

"I'm listening. What did you have in mind?"

# Chapter 3

## Amy

## February 14th 2017

My mom gave me the kind of reassuring smile that wouldn't have convinced the most gullible person on the planet. She said maybe she'd win big at bingo that night and this would be a big fuss over nothing.

That was a long shot if ever I heard one. I didn't know if the top prize at the local bingo ran into the hundreds of thousands of dollars, but I doubted that too.

My mind was whirling with a million questions a second, most of which were some variation of "What are we going to do?"

All I wanted was to be wrapped up in a protective hug while somebody else sorted everything out. My mom's defeated smile told me she couldn't be that person right now. I couldn't burden her with my own worries on top of what she was already feeling, so I gave her a smile that was probably a mirror image of hers.

I finished the dishes in a daze and then went to my room to call Anthony. Five missed calls and voicemails later, I shoved my phone in my pocket and leaned forward against the wall with my head resting on my forearm.

My fingers stroked the surface of the wall while something inside of me seemed to wind up more tightly by the second. A single sob burst out of me and I adjusted my position to muffle my mouth and stop any more coming out, but it was a losing battle.

This was more than just some wood and nails sitting on some dirt. There was *history* here. There was a photo album in the living room with some of the oldest pictures you could imagine showing my Great-Great-Grandfather building this house when he was a young man.

Some people might have thought it was stupid, but I swore I could feel the generations of memories flowing through this house. It had kept my family warm, dry and safe for over a hundred years and we were going to lose it on *my* watch?

I pushed myself off the wall and wiped my eyes, heading back to the kitchen and pulling the car keys off the hook. My mom looked up from the bank notice glumly.

"I need to go out for a bit," I said. "Have fun at bingo."

"Aren't you going on a date with Anthony tonight?"

"Yeah, I'll be back in time to get ready, not sure if I'll be back before you go out with Agnes though."

It was a lie. All my plans for my big night were out the window. All I wanted for Valentine's Day was to be held and to have somebody to hide my face against.

One day to hide from the world with somebody who cared for me. That's all I needed. If Anthony could just look after me for tonight, I could start thinking my way out of this mess tomorrow. I was sure of it.

He lived on the east edge of town, the side nearest our farm, and had been working at his dad's custom furniture business for the past several months since graduation. As the boss's son, he was allowed pretty flexible hours, and he'd said he was taking the afternoon off to make sure everything was organized for our big Valentine's date.

The last thing I was expecting to see when I pulled into the driveway was a little sports car with the license plate number 'SH3LLZ' parked behind Anthony's pickup. I recognized it, of course; it belonged to Rochelle, one of the most popular girls from my school.

I thought she was off at college living the sorority sister high life, so I had no idea what she was doing back in town, let alone at my boyfriend's house. On Valentine's Day.

She was always a little too friendly with Anthony for my liking, but he assured me there was nothing going on, they'd just known each other since they were five. I may have been a little unsure of myself as far as being a girlfriend went, but I didn't want to be *that* type, making false accusations all the time, so I said I believed him.

The way her car was here out of the blue on today of all days made me go numb, though. Maybe all the smoke I'd been breathing for the last couple of years really did mean there was a fire.

When I stepped out of the car I didn't close the door behind me. Something told me that this might very well be a time for stealth.

I walked up the path and had to consciously uncurl my hands, which had bunched up into tight little balls of stress that forced my fingernails into my palms painfully. After climbing the steps, I stood at the front door and I felt like I was marching into a gas chamber.

"Please don't do this to me today," I said. "Please, please, please not today."

With my hand raised, ready to knock, I heard a sharp sound to my right, coming through the window that I knew looked into their living room. I took a step towards it.

*Get back in your car and leave, you don't want to see this.*

I ignored my internal monologue and took another step. Inch by inch, the room was revealed to me. I saw the back of Anthony's head, sitting low on the couch facing away from the window. He wasn't wearing a shirt.

Another step showed that he wasn't wearing pants either. Rochelle was there, also facing away from the window, straddling Anthony and bouncing on his erection.

Around her midriff was a red ribbon tied into a bow at her lower back that bounced along with her. There was some writing on it in white text, the part I could see read "ppy Valen" and I could fill in the blanks no problem.

Anthony slapped her on the ass; it was the sound that I'd heard a few seconds ago. Slowly, as if I was still in stealth-mode, I crumpled to my knees. They disappeared over the horizon of the window sill, then I leaned forward and buried my face in my hands.

Fresh tears came. My heart was broken. My *life* was broken. The horrific echoes of taunting and laughter from my last few days at my old school came back to me, and blasted away my illusions again, leaving me with the same self-loathing I'd been running from for the past two years.

*You deserve this, you brought it on yourself. What? You thought you were worth waiting for? You're a sick* sick *girl and nobody will ever love you.*

I crawled back in the direction of the door so they wouldn't see me if they'd changed positions, then stood, and returned to the car. As I pulled away, I saw their faces looking out at me from the window.

# Chapter 4

# Kris

# March 2017

"Here it is," said Kevin, "I know an agency called InnocenceForSale.com that auctions off girls' virginities, and their terms and conditions offer an interesting opportunity for me to make some money off of you."

Daniel and I shared an incredulous glance at each other before turning back to Kevin. "You can't be serious," I said.

"Oh, I am. What's the matter? Scared? I haven't even told you the terms of the bet yet."

I leaned back with my beer and moved my finger in forward circles, gesturing for him to go ahead and tell me, even though I was sure this was a joke.

"OK, I know that look, but trust me, it's real. I used it myself and it was the best week of my life."

I laughed hesitantly. "What are you doing paying for sex with some chick who nobody else wanted to get in bed with?"

"It's not like that, man," Kevin said. "I don't know where or how they find these girls, but Cindy over there is a troll compared to the one I won in the auction on this site."

I craned my neck over the back of the seat and looked at the beautiful model for a second. "*She's* a troll, huh? Guess that explains why she hits so hard, right Dan?"

Kevin and I laughed, even Daniel couldn't resist a chuckle.

"Only in *comparison*," said Kevin. "I paid a little over six hundred thousand and I'm telling you it was a fucking bargain."

"Six hundred *thousand* for pussy?" Daniel spluttered.

"Yep." Kevin took a sip of his drink.

"What does all this have to do with me?" I asked.

"There's an auction closing tonight, in about an hour. I've come prepared and I've already had preliminary access for you approved by the owner of the agency."

"What the fuck would I need this for?" I asked.

"You don't need it, but you're gonna *want* it. That's what I'm counting on. The whole wager *depends* on it."

"What do you mean?"

Kevin pulled out his phone and unlocked it before handing it to me. It showed an auction page with a countdown timer, a picture of an admittedly stunning young woman named Amy, listed her various physical attributes, a little sales pitch about her, a laundry list of sex acts she was willing to participate in, and showed the current bid at almost five hundred thousand dollars.

I flicked through her gallery of photos, which showed her in various poses and a couple different outfits, before the slideshow went back to the main picture, a close up of her face. She had a beautiful smile and those baby-blue eyes were out of this world. I handed his phone back.

"OK, she's hot as hell," I conceded. "What do I have to do?"

Kevin smiled like a fisherman who feels a nibble. "Basically, what I had in mind was for you to win the auction for a start, then the girl stays with you for a week *but* you have to resist the urge to fuck her, and send her back at the end of the week *still* a virgin. If you can do that then the agency will refund your money *and* I'll match the winning bid. If you *can't*, and let's face it, you can't, then your bid is obviously gone, but you also have to pay *me* whatever the winning bid was."

My mind looked at the situation from a few angles for a second. "Pfff, easiest money I ever fucking made-"

"Not so fast, cowboy. There's a bunch of fine print."

"Fuck sake, how much time have you spent thinking this through?"

"A few weeks, to be honest. Once the idea came to me, it was too perfect to let go."

"Alright, lay out the fine print."

Kevin smirked. "Well, first of all, you can't just meet her at the airport, tell her to have a nice week and then fuck off to the Bahamas until she's gone. You've got to spend at least twelve hours a day with her, and some of that time, you've got to be alone. In bed asleep doesn't count, and I'll even cut you a little bit of slack and say you can sleep in separate rooms."

"That's very generous of you," I said.

"I know. Second, and this is a big one, you can't fuck any other girl from now until the week is up."

"From *now*?"

Kevin nodded.

"How long does it take for the girl to show up after the auction closes?"

"Could be a month or more, the agency will have to check you out before they send the girl and make sure you're not a serial killer with the clap."

"How many serial killers' weapon of choice is the clap?" I muttered, then spoke up. "A *month*?"

"Or more."

"I haven't gone that long without since I was fifteen," I said.

"And then you'll have to spend a week with what will probably be the hottest girl you've ever seen," Kevin laughed.

The girl on Kevin's phone was cute as fuck, but that was probably an exaggeration on his part. Still, even if she was half as good as her pictures, by the time I'd abstained from sex for a month, I'd probably be delirious with lust.

I took another sip of my drink and drummed my fingers on the table. Maybe something like this would be good for me. It could be like a sex-detox process. I mean, here I was in this club, surrounded by beautiful women, with a sexy girl's phone number written on a card in my pocket and I didn't give a fuck about any of them anymore.

If I forced myself to go without for a while, maybe I could recapture the kind of feelings I used to have, bringing home a new girl every time I hit the town. I stroked my cheek.

"So, the moment this girl is out of my sight through the departure gates at the airport at the end of the week, I can grab an air hostess and fuck her on one of those luggage scales?"

"Of course."

"Any other fine print?" I asked.

"Just have a little class. Don't intentionally make her despise you, and no jerking off while the girl is living with you," said Kevin.

"Uh... how do you plan to keep track of all this?" asked Daniel. "You setting up a jerk-off cam in his bedroom?"

"Nah, I trust him. He'd rather lose the bet than win by lying about it," said Kevin.

"OK... what about if she sucks me off, but I don't fuck her? You should pay up double in recognition of my supreme willpower, right?"

Kevin laughed. "No! This is all about the ever-fucking Kris Lane keeping his dick out of this girl. I don't think there's any way you can do it. Tell you what, though. If you blow a load down her throat but don't fuck her, I won't pay you anything, but you don't have to pay me anything either. I'll leave it up to you to argue with Ada, she runs Innocence For Sale, about getting your bid back. Deal?"

I held up my hands and smiled. "You might as well write the check now, shit for brains. I'm in."

Kevin held out his hand and I shook it. Kevin turned to Daniel. "Witness?"

"Witness!"

"Alright." Kevin pulled out his phone again and tapped away at it. "I've sent you an access link"

Sure enough, the message from Kevin was there when I unlocked my own phone. I clicked it and found myself on the site Kevin had showed me. A moment later, I had navigated through to Amy's auction page. The bid was already at five hundred and fifty thousand, and the countdown showed half an hour to go.

"You driving the price up on this auction?" I asked.

"Nope… but that wouldn't matter to you anyway, would it?"

I shrugged. "More money for me."

I entered a bid of seven hundred and sixty thousand in the hope of scaring off the other bidders. On the other side of the table, Kevin and Dan looked at Kevin's phone.

"Seven sixty, that you?" Daniel asked.

"Yeah."

For several minutes, it looked like my plan had worked, but then I saw the bid tick over to eight hundred thousand.

"Fuck."

I put in a bid of eight hundred and fifty thousand, but almost immediately somebody countered with nine hundred thousand.

"I think this is a record, I'm not sure," said Kevin.

I submitted a bid of nine hundred and fifty thousand, hoping whoever I was bidding against was feeling the looming pressure of the million-dollar mark. It wasn't *that* much more than what we'd already committed to, but there's just something about that number that feels different.

There was less than ten minutes left on the countdown when the bid updated to nine hundred and seventy five thousand dollars. That was a smaller increment than they'd been bidding before, so my hunch about the million-dollar mark was right.

Kevin wasn't joking when he said he had a wager that wasn't under-the-sofa-cushions bullshit. This was some serious money he was going to be paying me.

The bid updated to nine hundred and eighty nine thousand dollars, then a second later all the way up to nine hundred and ninety nine thousand, where it stayed until the countdown showed fifty nine seconds left.

"Is that you?" Kevin asked.

"No. Looks like there's at least two others bidding for her."

"You out?"

"No."

Forty five seconds. I entered one million and ten thousand dollars, then clicked submit. The million dollar barrier was broken.

Thirty seconds. The bid updated to one million and fifty… then one million and eighty thousand dollars.

Ten seconds. I entered one million one hundred and eighty thousand dollars, feeling my heart pounding about thirty beats every time the screen flickered with the countdown animation.

Three. Two. One… Finalizing. It still showed my bid. A minute later my phone buzzed and an email had come through congratulating me on my winning bid. I slumped back and took a deep breath.

"I won."

"It's on?" asked Kevin.

"It's on." I fished the card with Lacey's number on it out of my pocket and flicked it across the table at Daniel. "Guess I won't be needing that. See what you can do with it."

What had I just gotten myself into?

# Chapter 5

# Amy

# May 2017

The fasten-seat-belt lights switched off and sparked a commotion of metallic clacking as everybody stood and started opening the overhead compartments to recover their carry-on luggage. Everybody except me, that is.

I stared straight ahead at the little screen set into the back of the seat in front of me, which read "Welcome to New Eastport" with little fireworks animations popping off in the background. If my stomach was to be believed, then I was part of an interstate butterfly-smuggling operation.

My hands rested numbly on top of my bare thighs. The dress I was wearing was short enough to be enticing but long enough to be classy. Ada, the woman who ran InnocenceForSale.com, had it down to a fine science. For my height, this was the perfect length to drive men wild.

I'd found the site before the end of February at the end of a long night searching the internet for money-making schemes. I'd seen an article about a girl who sold her virginity for big bucks, and then tentatively looked for sites that handled those kind of... transactions.

That's what I was now. Something that had been bought and sold for some man's pleasure. By the end of the night a rich, possibly octogenarian, man would have taken my virginity and cum inside me.

A lump formed in my throat, possibly made out of the last remnants of my illusions about the way my first time was supposed to be. None of that mattered anymore. I had a job to do. I swallowed it away, cleared my throat and stood to retrieve my own carry-on.

I clutched my bag against my body like a shield, lost in my own world and trying to ignore the way everybody was looking at me. The men's eyes darted all over my body. The women's eyes did too, but they were narrowed angrily and darted back and forth between me and their partners.

I wasn't used to this kind of attention. Growing up on the farm, I'd never really thought much about the kind of working-over Ada's team gave me. Every square inch of my body, and I mean *every* square inch, had been fussed over by an expert in their field.

It was all part of the package for the winning bidder, to have the perfect sex object delivered to them. Ada explained it was also for me, to help boost my confidence in what was an unavoidably nerve-wracking situation. I didn't think it was working.

My face burned and I held my bag even tighter, staring at the heels of the person in front of me as we shuffled along the aisle towards the door. The head of the flight cabin crew was personally thanking and welcoming every passenger to New Eastport as we stepped off the plane into the mobile tunnel leading into the airport.

I welcomed the breeze that hit me from the gap between the tunnel and the side of the plane, cooling my flushed face. My thoughts drifted to the same ones that had kept me awake more and more since my auction closed.

Who was this man who had paid over a million dollars to take my virginity? What *kind* of a man did that?

Despite Ada's reassurances that her clients weren't the type that had any problems picking up women, it was hard to believe. That's where my fears about him being an octogenarian sprang from, those quiet times at night failing to sleep.

Despite that fear, I still boarded the plane and here I was. I would do it, even *that*, even for a *week*, to save the farm.

Lost in my thoughts, I followed the flow of people from my plane through the airport to the baggage reclaim area. With a luggage trolley gripped in my hands, I staked a claim to a clear spot near the conveyor belt and waited.

It took several minutes before it started moving, and I used the time to try to remember everything from Ada's crash course on being an IFS girl. She would have liked to spend more time preparing me, but I insisted everything happen as quickly as possible.

I had the bank's looming deadline terrorizing me into that insistence and even so it had still been over a month and a half since my auction closed. If everything worked out, I'd be paid *just* in time to clear the mortgage and save the farm.

Luggage of all shapes and sizes began parading past me while I waited. I tugged the hem of my dress down and looked at the modest neckline, which barely hinted at my small chest.

For some reason, I'd expected Ada to accentuate what little I had in that department a lot more, but as usual she had a reasoned answer for everything. I wasn't a slut, the client could have picked up one of those for a couple hundred bucks. I wasn't a high-end escort, you could get those for a thousand or two. I wasn't even a celebrity porn star. You could pick those up for less than five figures.

I was an IFS girl, and I was worth a record-breaking seven figures. The only girls worth that much were pure, innocent, natural beauties, and sometimes less is more.

The remembered sound of Anthony's hand smacking Rochelle's ass cut that train of thought off before it was in any danger of going to my head. *He* didn't think I was worth much. The boyfriend before that had driven me out of school.

I sighed. One man's trash is another man's treasure, I supposed. Suddenly, I realized that the conveyor belt was almost devoid of luggage, and the crowd of fellow passengers was almost gone, while other planeloads gathered at other reclaim areas.

My sad and lonely suitcase bumped along and I reached out for it, before letting it go past one more time. I reached into my pocket and pulled out a jewelry-case. Inside was a simple and tasteful gold and "diamond" necklace, which was really some crazy high-tech gadget with a built in GPS and panic button.

If I was in trouble and I pressed it, apparently, the cavalry would come charging in wherever I was. They were supposed to be with me already, professionals in the background so as not to interfere with the client's encounter as long as he didn't do anything without my consent.

I looked around and didn't see anybody in dark suits holding their finger against their ear and speaking into covert microphones while staring at me through sunglasses. If the client, Kris, asked me, I was supposed to say the necklace was a family heirloom and I never took it off.

My luggage came around again shortly after I'd managed to wrestle with the clasp and arrange the necklace to it was sitting nicely. Bracing myself, I heaved the heavy suitcase off the conveyor belt with a grunt.

"You need some help with that?"

I looked over at the young man who had sprung up out of nowhere as I waddled back to my trolley.

"No. No thank you," I said, with a strained voice.

It took all of my strength to get the bag high enough to get it on, but I managed it.

"You just arrive home, or just visiting?" he asked.

"Uh, visiting."

"Oh, really? Could I get your number? I'd could show you around or something?"

"Uh... um... well... no. Sorry, you seem nice and everything but I'm... you know... I'm with somebody else."

I braced myself for some version of a "you think you're too good for me or something?" insult, feeling as awkward as those dreams where you realize you've gone to school naked. Ada told me that for this week, I had to act as if Kris was the only man in the world. The other men were *people* who just kind of existed, but Kris was the only *man*.

She had asked me to give her an example of how I politely decline a male's advances, because the situation might come up while I was with Kris. The look on her face would have been funny if it hadn't been directed at me while I stammered my way through some cliché.

The truth was, I'd never really said no before. Imagine that, a virgin who never said no. I'd been in two long-term, for my age, relationships and in school everybody just kind of knows you're with somebody so I'd basically only been asked out those two times.

The insult never came. "Oh, OK, well, have a good time. Sorry for bothering you."

"It was no…"

He waved his hand and cut me off, already turning away. I took a deep breath and let it out slowly with my cheeks puffed up, then pushed my trolley towards the exit.

*Oh my gosh, oh my gosh, oh my gosh… aaaahhhhhhh!*

My nerves made it almost impossible to think of anything useful, and I leaned on the trolley as much as I could to make up for how weak I felt in the knees. The doors slid open and I paused as a spotlight hit me and crowd of people stared.

They weren't all there for me, of course, they were there to meet their friends, family and business associates, but for a second I felt the weight of all their eyes as if they knew why I was here. The spotlight was just the setting sun, shining in through the floor-to-ceiling glass at the front of the airport terminal. I had to look down at my feet for a second before the sensation passed and I could move forward again.

After a couple of steps, I scanned the crowd. Some people were holding up signs.

*Jim Smith.*
*Hayley Atkins – Gibraltar Conference.*
*Amy – IFS*

My heart leapt into my throat, making an emergency dash toward my brain to throw the whole thing in reverse. Then I looked at the face above the sign, and my heart stayed where it was.

Our eyes locked and I took the last few steps towards him without even feeling the weight of the trolley or my own body. I stopped in front of him, on the other side of the temporary barrier, and looked up.

His eyes were deep-brown and set in the most gloriously perfect face I'd ever seen. He was sporting a hint of stubble, short enough to look professional, but visible enough that something made me want to reach out and stroke his cheek.

Even without touching him, I could imagine how that stubble would feel against my soft skin, the way it would tickle my neck if he hugged me. Maybe he had a stubble consultant the way I had a skirt-length consultant.

His broad shoulders and thick arms filled out his suit like nobody's business, and tattoos peeked out from the collar and cuffs. It was an intoxicating contrast.

I felt so small next to him, like he could pick me up and throw me without any effort at all. I'd never encountered such a dominating presence before. If I was supposed to pretend that Kris was the only man in the world, I was in trouble.

"Um... hi? I'm Amy. Are you the... driver?" I spoke as quietly as I could, not wanting anybody else to hear our exchange.

The corner of his mouth raised a little. "No. I'm Kris."

*Whaaaaat?*

I blinked, and bit my tongue on the suggested response from the voice in my head. "Oh! I'm Amy... uh... I said that already... well... sorry... it's nice to meet you."

*Great first impression!*

That wasn't the *exact* wording I'd been practicing, but it was all I had. I watched my hand reach up towards him as if it belonged to somebody else.

It was absurd to think I was in a position to touch him. He was the kind of guy you might giggle about with your friends as he passed you on his way to his private jet, living in a whole other league of existence.

What he saw in little old me, I had no idea, but Ada said that it was important to initiate physical contact as soon as possible. I had to let the client know that it was OK to touch me, that I wanted him to get close to me.

I touched his neck, then curled my fingers around and pulled myself up to the tips of my toes. He bent down stiffly and let me plant a timid little kiss on his cheek. His stubble was every bit as tingly as I thought it would be against my lips, and he smelled like a cross between heaven and hard work.

"*Really* nice to meet you," I repeated.

# Chapter 6

# Kris

When the doors slid open I nearly forgot how to breathe. She stood there with those blue eyes wide open, catching the setting sun at just the right angle to make them look like they glowed with supernatural beauty.

I'd seen gorgeous women before. I'd seen women who turned every head in the room before. Hell, even Cindy turned heads that night I first laid eyes on Amy's picture.

What I *hadn't* seen before was a girl so beautiful that it made me *ache* to not be touching her. Maybe it was the month and a half of abstinence, but every flutter of her eyelash, curve of her face, the way her blonde hair bounced and the movement of her body almost physically pulled me to her.

Amy's eyes shot down as if she didn't know what to do with herself, and her youthful inexperience shone through. She was fucking adorable, and my two million plus dollars were in serious trouble.

I was immeasurably thankful for the few steps she took while looking at her feet, since it gave me a chance to regroup. By the time she looked up again, I felt more or less in charge of myself, but watching her move wasn't easy by any stretch of the imagination.

Her eyes caught the sign I was holding and then travelled up to meet my gaze. I could almost hear a click when our eyes locked. Fireworks could have gone off next to me and I wouldn't have turned to look at them.

The closer she stepped, the clearer it became how petite she was. She was *lucky* I was going to hold back this week, or I might break her in half. If I slid myself between those legs…

I swallowed as discreetly as I could and mentally shook myself while she stammered her way through an introduction and asked if I was the driver.

"No. I'm Kris."

"Oh! I'm Amy… uh… I said that already… well… sorry… it's nice to meet you."

She reached up and her thumb stroked my cheek before her fingers curled around the back of my neck and she pulled herself up on the tips of her toes. Even then she wasn't tall enough to reach me, so I bent down and she gave me the softest kiss the world had ever seen on my cheek.

"*Really* nice to meet you," she said.

Those lips. They were the stuff dreams were made of. I wanted to push her down to her knees and feed my hard cock past them, feel their velvet softness all around my shaft as her throat caressed the head… fucking hell.

"Nice to meet you too, Amy. We're parked that way." I pointed. "So head in that direction and I'll help you with that cart."

Amy nodded. "OK."

We walked parallel to each other, each of us spending just as much time looking at the other as we were looking where we were going. I met her where the barrier ended and took over pushing the cart for her, putting my sign in the little wire basket.

"Good flight?" I asked.

"Yeah, it was fine. Um… are you *sure* you're Kris?"

"Reasonably sure, yeah. They didn't tell you anything about me?"

"No, I was pretty sure you were a man, but that's all," she said.

"Guilty as charged. What were you expecting?" I asked.

She blushed a little, not the deep red of cataclysmic embarrassment, but enough to show the sincerity of her underlying nerves. They weren't lying when they said it was innocence for sale.

"Something," she paused, her eyes rolling up as if searching for the right words in her head. "Not as nice as you."

I grinned at her and the hopeful little smile on her own face blossomed into something angelic. It was hard to believe there were really women like her roaming around the world, untouched by man.

My driver, Bernard, saw us coming and stepped out of the car to open the back door, greeting the two of us with supreme professionalism. Once she was safely in the car, he took control of the luggage cart, wheeling it to the trunk, and I followed Amy into the back seat.

The way she watched me enter the car made it clear she was wondering if I was going to jump on top of her straight away and fuck her while we drove home. Her hands were braced on the seat and she didn't relax until I sat down on the opposite side to her right and put my seatbelt on. Even so, she was still tense.

Bernard shut the door behind us, hopped in the front on the other side of the soundproof glass, and we were on the move in a jiffy. Amy seemed to be wracking her brain for something to say.

"Don't worry, relax," I said. "You're safe, you're great. We don't need to rush anything."

She sighed, and unwound a little bit. "OK, thanks. I'm sorry, it's just so... weird. I've never done this before. Obviously."

"What made you decide to do it now?" I asked.

"Well... I've got my reasons."

"Oh, very coy. You ever been to New Eastport before?"

She shook her head.

"I've been here for ten years now, it's longer than I've lived anywhere else, so I suppose it's home."

I spent the rest of the car ride pointing out a few landmarks and giving her a bit of trivia about the place, and she relaxed even more as the journey progressed. The nerves did seem to return a little when we pulled into my building's parking garage.

Bernard dropped us off by the elevator and I waved away his offer to carry the bags. Amy followed me into the elevator and smoothed out her dress a little after catching a glimpse of herself in the mirrored walls.

She caught me looking at her legs, which her dress showed off wonderfully, and bit her bottom lip. I averted my eyes to the floor-readout when I felt my cock twitch in my pants.

The doors opened to a private hallway leading to the door of my penthouse suite. I lifted the bags again and made sure the bigger one was between us as we walked.

"Do you own this or rent?" she asked as we reached the door.

"I've got it on a five-year lease. I didn't want to buy the place, but I didn't want the hassle of being told I had to move unexpectedly either."

I pushed the door open and gestured for her to lead the way before picking up her bags again. She walked ahead slowly as if stepping through a portal into another world.

"Wow." Her head turned in every direction, taking it all in, then she rushed over to the window to look down on the city nightscape. "Look at this view!"

I'd seen what it looked like out those windows countless times, I was more interested in the girl standing in front of them. She turned back and saw me watching her, then took a deep breath and walked slowly in my direction.

"Your room's this way," I said, backing off before she got to me.

"OK."

Amy followed me to the room I'd had prepared for her, the furthest one from my room in the whole suite. I put her large suitcase down on the ground, and the smaller one on the bed itself.

When I turned around, Amy was right there. She placed her hands on my chest and then moved them to my sides as she stepped in close. She looked up at me with wide-eyed innocence and expectation.

I licked my lips and cleared my throat. "Take it easy, we've got all week. I don't know how far exactly you've come, so take some time to freshen up if you want. This room has an en suite bathroom there."

"Really?"

"Yeah, of course. Take some time to yourself and we can have some dinner in half an hour."

"Well... OK. Sure."

# Chapter 7

# Amy

Kris backed away from me, then circled around my suitcase to the door and closed it behind him, leaving me alone in the most luxurious bedroom I'd ever seen. When he'd said "Your room's this way" my mind had interpreted it as "Our room's this way" but, despite all the expensive comforts, this room lacked any signs of being lived in. It really was *my* room.

The carpet felt so wonderfully soft under my feet after I kicked my shoes off. I took my phone out of my bag and returned a message from my mom, who thought I was away for a week visiting a sick friend, then plugged it in to charge and turned on the temporary phone Ada had given me for the week.

I heard the faint clatter of Kris, presumably in the kitchen, as I knelt down by my suitcase and unzipped it. Inside was a mixture of some of my own clothes and some that Ada had provided, which included some evening wear, and some outfits that were for Kris' eyes only.

Nurse, secretary, cheerleader. I rushed to hang the more risqué items up and then push them to the back of the closet so I could hang up the regular clothes in front of them as if they were a dirty secret. Same for the lubricant, which I popped into the drawer of the bedside table.

That done, I let myself flop back on the bed. Was this it? Was *this* the bed I was going to lose my virginity in? Or was he going to take me in his room then... what? Send me back here?

This was so strange. Nothing had been like I'd expected and much had already strayed from Ada's general guidelines too.

She'd said that many clients met their girls at the airport with raging hard-ons and got down to business as soon as there was a semi-private area with a flat surface or sturdy wall to use. After that, the rest of the week tended to be more slow and sensual.

Not Kris though. He seemed almost reluctant to touch me. What if he didn't like me? The thought made my stomach sink so fast that I sat bolt upright again.

The idea was unthinkable. Right now, my mom was rolling around the house, packing up whatever she was able to because I couldn't bear to tell her why there was any reason to hope we could save the farm.

Surely he liked me? He saw my pictures and spent over a million dollars on me. I mean, the photos Ada had done were professional and made me look a lot better than real life, but after all the beauticians and stylists had worked me over, I hopefully wasn't the kind of fish you threw back into the ocean.

I took a deep breath and willed the knot out of my stomach. It was too early to be discouraged. The truth was in his eyes. He wanted me, but I guessed he was holding back to be a gentleman.

I came here willing to submit myself to a man a million times less attractive than Kris. I'd even ticked the box saying I was willing to work with a couple and I had no particular interest in other women. I could break the ice here. I could do this. The voice giving me the pep talk inside my head sounded a lot like Ada.

After checking myself in the bathroom mirror, I tentatively exited the room and followed the sounds and smells to where Kris was working in the kitchen. I walked up and rested my hands on the breakfast bar.

"Need any help?" I asked.

"No, don't worry. I made most of this earlier, there's not much to do now. Do you like to cook?"

"I don't mind it. I wouldn't say I'm fantastic, but I've never given anybody any food poisoning."

"Ah, my favorite kind of chef. Would you like some wine?"

"Well, maybe just one glass. Thank you." I smiled.

"Red? White? Rose?"

"Whatever you recommend, I'm not a connoisseur. I'll just be happy if it doesn't come in a cardboard box."

"Alright, I can manage that."

Kris turned the dial down on something on the stove and pulled a bottle of wine out of a wine fridge, tracked down a corkscrew and two glasses, then poured one for each of us. He handed me mine and held his up.

"To an amazing week," I said.

He paused for a moment, then clinked glasses and repeated the toast. I wasn't a big drinker, so I nursed my wine while I watched him cook.

About ten minutes later, he was holding my chair out for me at the dining table, which took in the spectacular views that had taken my breath away when I first entered the penthouse. The pile of pasta on my plate looked delicious.

"Yum, Italian is my favorite," I said.

"Me too."

"Is this what you do? Are you one of those celebrity chefs? Sorry if I should know that, I don't watch those shows."

"Me? Hell no, I'm amateur at best. I mean, like you, my food has never killed anybody, but I'm more a... serial entrepreneur. I build businesses from the ground up with a view to sell them after they're established."

"Really? How does that work?"

"How do you mean?"

"Well, I dunno, I guess it seems strange to sell a business that's working well. I assume they're working well when you sell them, I mean."

"Yep, you get a better price for those ones rather than a business that resembles a plane heading toward a mountain. It might be counterintuitive to a degree, but think about it like this. No company can ever replicate to the kind of growth it experiences when starting from scratch, if you know what you're doing from the start. I like to run businesses during periods of maximum growth, whatever business that may be."

I ate some of my pasta while I listened. "Mmm, it's good. I guess that makes sense."

"How about you? The site said you're a waitress and caregiver?"

"Yeah. I know it's not as glamorous as the other girls on there, but it's hard to find something else to do back home. I'm trying to find another job."

"Where *is* back home?" he asked.

"Um... sorry, I'm not supposed to say."

"Oh, right, well, what *kind* of job are you after?"

I laughed. "I'm open to suggestions. I like to draw, so if I could choose then I'd *love* to get into something in art or design."

"That's great. There's a lot of opportunities. In design, at least. I don't really know how the art world works."

"Hopefully."

"What kind of caregiver are you?"

"Oh, that's not exactly a job, but it takes up some of my time so Ada put it on there. I help out my mom because she's in a wheelchair. She's pretty self-sufficient, but needs help with some things, you know, we live out on a farm and not everything is perfectly smooth so sometimes she just needs somebody there to push her around."

"Your dad's not…?"

"He's not around," I said quietly.

"Sorry."

"It's OK."

Kris and I talked as we ate pasta and sipped wine. We seemed to be in a reverse-race to see who could make their single glass last the longest, as he made sure to not drink his any faster than me.

He was easy to talk to, which was another surprise for me given the situation and how much older than me he was. I tried to guess his age. Late thirties? A young-looking forty-something?

After we'd finished our food and had been talking for about an hour, I finished off the last sip of my wine and grew quiet, looking over at him on the other side of the table.

I lucked out here. Kris was a hypnotically handsome man with a wealth of experience. Maybe it was the wine talking, but he made me feel kind of funny, like some of the butterflies from the riot in my stomach had moved between my legs. All that and he was going to save my family's farm.

With a napkin, I dabbed at the corners of my mouth to make sure I wasn't about to do this with any hint of green pesto on my face. Setting it down, I took a deep breath and stood up before circling around the table.

Kris swiveled his body slowly to face me as I moved, my fingertips trailing along the edge of the table. Our eyes locked, like they had that first moment in the airport, and I sunk to my knees in front of him, pushing his legs apart.

I shuffled forward, resting my forearms on his thighs, feeling the taut muscles of his quads bulging there, and looked up at him. Under his intense gaze, I felt like I was already almost naked.

"I've never done this before, but I want to try, OK?" I asked, reaching for the zipper of his pants.

I looked down and my breath caught in my throat as I could plainly see the outline of his cock semi-hard down one leg of his pants. It clearly dwarfed what little I'd seen of Anthony's as it disappeared inside Rochelle.

With another gulp, I slowly continued to reach for his zip. Could I even open my mouth wide enough to take that?

The instant my finger touched his zip, Kris seemed to startle out of a trance. He grabbed my wrist and pulled my hand away.

"Hey, we've got all week. There's no need to rush things. Why don't we call it a night and we'll see each other early tomorrow?"

"Um… you… well, OK. If that's what you want. Uh… do you want some help with the dishes or something?"

"No, the maid will take care of it in the morning," he said.

Kris stood and helped me to my feet.  I held on to his hands, stopping him from pulling away, and put them on my hips.  His hands were so big I wondered how close he was to being able to make his fingertips and thumbs touch around my waist.

"You know it's OK to touch me, right?" I said.

"I know." His eyes were a window into a tempest of desire.

"Good.  Well, goodnight, Kris.  I can't wait to see you tomorrow."

Ada coached me on all the right things to say, but I really meant this one.

# Chapter 8

# Kris

After a night plagued by dreams about Amy, I worked out some frustrations in the building's gym and had the coldest shower I could handle. By the time I returned, the maid had been and gone but I didn't see any sign of Amy yet.

I dropped my bag and stood still for a moment. In the silence I could just make out the sound of the shower running in Amy's en suite. My mind tormented me by flashing images of beads of water running down her smooth, naked, body.

It didn't help knowing that I could just barge into that shower, grab her by her hair, throw her on the bed and fuck her to my heart's content. If I won this bet, I was going to have to come up with something that would make Kevin's life hell for a while to pay him back for this.

It was a fucking crime to have to send Amy away at the end of the week without having had my cock in her. I sat at the breakfast bar, poured a bowl of cereal grumpily and munched on it as if it was a voodoo doll in Kevin's image.

Behind me, the door to Amy's room opened. I looked around to see Amy walking in my direction, wearing a bathrobe. This was the first time in my life I'd ever considered a bathrobe sexy, and wished it hid more of her legs.

"Morning, can I join you?" she asked.

"Yeah, help yourself." I gestured at the box of cereal, milk and fruit. "I'll get you a bowl."

"No, don't get up. Where are they?"

"They're in that cupboard up there," I said.

Amy opened the cupboard and looked up at the stack of bowls. She had to rise to the tips of her toes and reach for them, which only served to make her bathrobe ride up higher.

I determinedly stared at my own breakfast, ignoring the voice in my head that was begging me to sweep all this food off the bench, lift her up and take her right here just to see what kind of sounds I could fuck out of her.

She managed to lift the top bowl off the stack and came back to the breakfast bar via the cutlery drawer. Using the spoon, she chopped a banana over her cereal and then poured on some milk.

"We've got a busy day today," I said.

Amy's jaw stopped moving mid-crunch, then slowly started up again. She swallowed hard and I realized what she must be thinking.

"No! Not... well, I mean, we're going to be out most of the day."

"Oh... doing what?" she asked.

"I've got most of the week off work, but there's a few really important events happening that I absolutely can't get around. You'll be my date for them. Got to keep up appearances, portray the right image. Some folks don't think you're successful if you haven't got a beautiful woman on your arm"

"You think I'm pretty enough?" she asked.

I snorted in disbelief. "You're pretty enough to make the other women give up and go home."

Amy beamed and quickly turned back to her food, but smiling and eating at the same time wasn't the easiest thing to do. After a few more mouthfuls, she looked at me again.

"What's happening today, then?"

"I'm entertaining a potential investor on my yacht today. It's disguised as a reward for a bunch of our highest-performing employees that we've invited him and his wife along to, but it's really all about him. He's this Texas oil tycoon type with old, *old*, money. My co-founder and I have been hoping he'll take the opportunity to buy us out completely, or almost completely."

"What should I wear?" Amy asked.

"It's casual." I paused and realized a great drawback of this social engagement today. "You like to swim? People tend to try out the jacuzzi or jump off the back to swim in the ocean."

"Yeah, I like to swim, sure."

"Got a swimsuit?" I hoped, if she did, it was one of those old-fashioned ones that were basically a swimming-kimono, complete with a cap for her hair.

"Yeah, I've got a couple bikinis and a sarong. One probably wouldn't be good for this, the other is pretty standard. Is that OK?"

"That'll be fine."

"When do we leave?"

"Straight after breakfast," I said.

"Oh. Alright."

*****

Any hopes I had that maybe Amy didn't look good in a bikini were smashed shortly after I helped her on board and introduced her to a few people. Kevin was there, of course, and my voodoo cereal didn't appear to have done much damage to him.

After introducing her, Kim from customer service and Jane from accounts receivables immediately wanted to drag her off to the jacuzzi so they could be the first in. That was fine by me; I needed to call Kevin an asshole in private anyway.

I just hoped Amy had her story down. It was pretty simple, we went over it in the car on the way. We met in a club, she's from out of town visiting a friend, she's a freelance designer. Keep it simple.

"You don't mind, do you?" Amy asked.

"No, go ahead. Towels are by the hot tub, you can leave your stuff anywhere you want in the meantime."

"OK, see you in a bit then."

Amy pulled her shirt off and untied her sarong. Either the world stopped for a moment, or the way everyone and everything including the slap of the ocean against the dock went silent was all in my head.

The black bikini was far from the scandalously-micro end of the scale. It was even a little conservative, if that could ever be said of a bikini, but she rocked it. She fuckin' *rocked* it.

While her eyes were distracted by the task of removing her outer layer of clothes, I couldn't help but take her all in. Without the wedge style shoes she'd been wearing at the airport, she struck me as even more petite than I'd first thought, with a slim body that was perfectly in proportion to her height.

When the sarong came off, I saw she had a scar on her thigh, or rather, several of them in a cluster. In all honesty, I was glad to see them.

Not because I reveled in her pain or any kind of bullshit like that. It simply meant she was human after all, and it wasn't like it was enough to knock her down from the perfect ten she'd been advertised as.

She put her clothes in a shoulder bag and put it on a seat, before rising to kiss me on the cheek. When she did that, her firm breasts hugged my arm for a moment, and then she was off with Kim and Jane. I jerked my head to the side and Kevin followed me to a clear area with a smug look on his face.

"This isn't fair," I said.

"I know. I think after all these years losing bets, purely to lure you into a false sense of security, I'm gonna to get *paid*."

"Think you've been playing the long game, huh? No chance, fucker. I'm starting to enjoy this kind of life, think I might become a monk after we sell up," I lied.

"Speaking of which, where is that cowpoke?" asked Kevin.

I laughed and nudged him with my elbow, then pointed at a long white car approaching the dock. It even had a set of horns on the hood as an ornament.

"Now, who could that be?" I said.

The potential new owner of Obvius.ly, Anson Allen, followed his wife out of the back of the car. If I didn't know better, I would have said he wore the same outfit every day, but the reality was he probably had dozens of the same cowboy boots, hats and everything in between.

"Morning, Anson, Elly," I said, helping Elly Allen on board.

"Howdy. Thanks again for the invite, much appreciated. I'm lookin' forward to talkin' to some of the staff, get a feel for what the company looks like from their perspective. Maybe then I can get the real dirt, huh?"

"You're welcome to try," I said. "Everybody here knows their job inside out, so you'll get to know all the different parts of the business at least, even if it doesn't get too dirty."

"Well, I'll look forward to that."

We set off for a leisurely cruise around, and not too far out of, the harbor. Everything was going great, even if the Allens did look a little out of place amongst the younger demographic typically employed in a tech startup.

Then Amy came back briefly and I introduced her as my date, before her new best friends Kim and Jane took her away again. Anson was polite enough while Amy was there, but after she left, he had a look on his face like somebody about to give a fatherly lecture.

"Everything OK, Anson?" I asked.

"Well, son, somethin's been botherin' me."

"What's that?"

"I couldn't put my finger on it until just now. Every time we've met outside of the office, you've had a different lady on your arm."

"And?"

"The way a man is in life is the way he is in business. You can't commit to a woman, how do I know you committed in the business? Always distracted by something shiny and new so you never see anything through to the end? That little lady is the shiniest. She looks like the newest too, she must be half your age."

"With all due respect, Anson, I keep my personal and business lives separate."

"Well, that may be. You might be the first person that ever managed it."

"My track record speaks for itself."

"Well, that may be," he repeated. "I'm tryin' to be open-minded about everything. That's why I came all the way out here, left home, to invest in somethin' *different*, but sometimes I feel like maybe I ain't a good fit for this kind of business." He gestured at a bikini-clad manager of social-media-marketing jumping off the side of the boat.

On the outside, I tried to remain calm. On the inside it was like a military command bunker that had just received news about World War III starting.

The Allen family, and all that sweet old black-gold money, were the only potential buyers we were currently courting that could reach into their deep pockets and swoop in on the business without endless boardroom and shareholder debates. Their money, once split amongst our shareholders, would push me into that fabled *billionaire* realm.

"Look, at its core, this business is like any business you've been involved with. We have suppliers, we have customers, and we keep track of all the same numbers for the same reasons. On some level, every business is the same thing with a different skin on it. Look at it like that and you'll see Obvius.ly is *thriving*."

I waved my hand around to gesture at the floating party. "This is just the skin. Customers subscribing to an app through a phone in their pocket is just the skin. You don't want to go back to Texas, where they've got a copy of the financial documents, and try to explain how the flashing lights and the bells and whistles of a tech startup was too much for the Allen family. Come on. You *know* your way around a business."

Anson mulled it over while a hush swept over the military command bunker in my brain. Soldiers, clutching gas masks, looked up anxiously. A General held his breath waiting to see what number he should write next to the word 'DEFCON.'

# Chapter 9

# Amy

After the all-day schmoozing-cruise was over, I thought we'd head back to Kris' penthouse, but instead he instructed the captain of the boat to take us to the other side of the harbor for dinner. My protests about having not packed anything for a dinner date were quashed, when he told me everything I needed was already in the bedroom below deck.

A sleek black evening gown, matching shoes and purse were laid out for me. Everything fit as snuggly as Cinderella's glass slipper.

I even felt like the girl from that fairytale when he offered me his arm and we walked along the waterfront, looking out at the water while the sun set behind us. He'd changed while I was down below and looked every inch the success that he clearly was.

I'd never had dinner at a restaurant where the staff addressed me by name before, nor had I eaten a plate of food that might have been a work of art. The best thing about it, though, was that they still had the option of plain old ice cream for dessert. Kris ordered ice cream too, but went for triple chocolate over my cookies and cream.

"So you're seriously going to sell Obvius.ly?" I asked. "I know you said you like to sell after the period of maximum growth... but aren't there any exceptions? I mean... *everybody's* heard of Obvius.ly, it's a big deal."

I took a spoonful of ice cream and Kris licked his lips as he watched me slip it into my mouth, then raised his eyes to mine. "Sure, there are exceptions. If you're especially passionate about the business in question, the specific way it generates revenue, then that's a factor. I'm more passionate about the business of business growth, though. That's just me. I've got too many ideas to just do one thing."

"Where do all these ideas come from? Like Obvius.ly... how did you know how to do all that?

"It came from my own frustration. I was using all these services on my phone, from calling rides to booking everything you can imagine, and so often one service or another would fuck up and have to reschedule, leaving me to try to shift everything that was pre-booked. I thought there must be an easier way. Obvius.ly 'talks' to all these different apps and does all the scheduling automatically. Movie almost done? Boom, the car you ordered is waiting for you afterwards, even if the start of the movie was delayed for some reason, and the restaurant you booked has been notified of the delay too."

"Yeah, one of my friends used it for a big day in the city for her birthday, said it was awesome. I missed it because I had to work. I wish I had come up with it! Or something else, but I never had an idea I thought would sell."

"You'd be surprised what would actually work if you built the business the right way. Kevin and I, my co-founder you met on the yacht today, once had a little wager between us to see who could build a business to the strongest position in just two months."

"What kind of businesses?" I asked.

"Ah, *that's* where the challenge was. We found a random word generator on the internet and clicked on it ten times each. From those ten words, we had to pick any combination of them to determine what the business did. Kevin got 'Incredible Herring Machine' and I got 'Annoying Instrument Jamming.'"

I laughed and almost choked on my ice cream. "What?"

"Yeah, I thought I had it in the bag, but he's a wily one, that Kevin. We had a one thousand dollar budget each to get them off the ground."

"Sounds like a good way to lose a thousand dollars, no?"

"Potentially, but they were both profitable after two months. I envisioned that poor bastard hiring vending machines and filling them with canned fish, but he ended up finding and buying a cheap patent for some fishing gadget that somebody never did anything with, then started selling it like there was no tomorrow."

"And what did you do?"

"I created a service that brought together tutors of unusual instruments with students whose friends all already knew how to play the guitar and who wanted to learn something different."

"Who won?" I asked.

"I did. His business model was more difficult to scale, with the manufacturing requirements and everything he had to pay for up front, whereas I was profitable almost straight away. Those were the youngest businesses we ever sold. I still look them up every now and then and they're both still around."

I sighed. A business like that would have made all the difference for us at some point in the last few years.

"Not doing as well as Obvius.ly though?"

"Nope, and you can get a demo of the app tomorrow, we're using it to have a nice day out."

"Oh, cool. You're keeping us busy, eh?"

"Sure am."

"What else do you have in store?" I asked.

"The big event is this Friday, we're having an office party for hitting twenty million monthly active users. I've got to go into the office on Wednesday morning, too. Other than that, well, we'll think of something."

I knew what that "something" might be, and swallowed a spoonful of ice cream slowly while picturing it. I'd push his jacket off. He'd slide the straps of my dress off my shoulders while I unbuttoned his shirt and then he'd hold me against his hard body.

My breasts would press against his tattooed muscles and he'd steer us towards the bed as we kissed, or maybe he'd pick me up. After that, I'd be completely at his mercy. He'd be inside me, claiming me.

I remembered the size of the bulge showing through his pants last night and wondered what it would be like to lose my virginity to that. Could I even handle it? Wild horses couldn't stop me from trying, but what would it be *like*?

"Can I have a taste of yours?" I asked.

"Sure."

Kris dipped his spoon into his bowl and held it out in my direction. As slowly as I dared, I let the ice cream into my mouth and slid it off the spoon with my lips, closing my eyes.

"Mmmm. Maybe I made the wrong choice."

When I opened my eyes again, Kris was looking at me with a mildly pained expression. Clearly the ice cream wasn't sating whatever hunger he was feeling right now.

"I think we should get the bill," he said.

"Good idea."

# Chapter 10

# Kris

Fuck the bet, fuck the two million three hundred and sixty thousand motherfucking dollars. She was worth it. I *needed* to feel her pussy wrapped around me.

I followed her into the car and, just like when I picked her up from the airport, she was ready for me, only this time she looked eager rather than completely on-edge. Closing the door behind me before Bernard could do it, I reached out for her and curled my fingers around the back of her neck, pulling her into a kiss.

Her lips were soft and kissed me back with enthusiasm as her arms wrapped around me so her hands could rest on my back. Bernard entered the driver's side, safely behind the soundproof barrier again, and started the car.

As if she'd been holding back for the cover of the engine, she let out a soft moan when our lips parted for a moment. She sounded like she was quietly admiring a pile of kittens that she'd never be allowed to cuddle.

I let my hands wander, finally feeling her slim shape under the palms of my hands through her evening gown. The material hugged her closely, allowing me to feel her every twitch and caught breath as I moved my hands to her hips, then slid one down to her leg.

"Yes," she breathed.

I broke off our kiss to lick and suck along her jawline until I reached her neck. Amy raised her chin and shivered as I kissed her just under her earlobe and then down the side of her neck.

The perfume I'd chosen smelled like it was made for her, like a limited-edition fragrance for royalty, with a hint of sunscreen underneath from her time on the yacht today. After several minutes of bumping along the road, she rose to her knees on the seat, then bunched her dress up around her thighs so she could straddle me.

My hands moved to her ass and squeezed tight, pulling her pussy closer to my cock, which was aching for release. I swore I could feel the heat of her virginal slit radiating through her panties, teasing my manhood with its closeness.

Her fingers ran through the hair at the back of my head, while her other hand stroked my cheek, cradling my head as we kissed. Our tongues touched and gently twirled, and Amy's kissing slowed as she learned the steps to this new dance.

She seemed to melt into me, her body draped over mine and making contact from chest to just above the waist. I was moving my hands behind her knees, seeking to widen her stance even further and close the distance there too, when Bernard turned the car into the parking garage.

The two of us tumbled out of the car and into the elevator. After I pushed the button, Amy slipped her arms around me inside my jacket and rested her cheek against my chest, closing her eyes.

I caught sight of us in the mirror. She looked so happy and content, it was all too easy to forget the seven figures of cash it took to get her here. I looked pretty happy too, which only served to remind me about the seven figures of cash *I* had on the line.

Fucking hell. I couldn't let Kevin win. The money, though a big enough sum to put a smile on Amy's face, was inconsequential in the face of the deal we hoped to close with Anson Allen. The part that was impossible to swallow was the thought of losing the bet. That would make it two in a row and it wasn't a trend I liked the sound of.

The elevator doors opened and Amy held my arm as we walked back to my penthouse. This was dangerous territory. I had a rock-hard cock, a willing virgin, and probably an hour more I needed to spend with Amy today to satisfy the terms of the bet.

I closed the door behind us while Amy held one hand and, once done, she grabbed the other too, and walked backwards, leading me inside. Her eyes held mine, then roamed over my body and back up again.

She was nervous beyond belief, expectant, turned on, all rolled into one cacophony of emotions that was playing like a movie in her eyes. I wanted her so fucking badly, to *take* what I paid for and turn up the volume on the moans she'd uttered in the car.

I needed a distraction. Any distraction.

"You want to watch a movie?" I asked, inspired by what I saw in her gaze.

"No, I've got a better idea."

"Well... how about we..."

"Don't you want to hear my idea?" she asked.

"Uh... OK."

Amy took a few deep breaths as she worked herself up to it. "I... it's part of the terms and conditions of Innocence For Sale." She blushed, but persevered with her explanation. "You get to... inspect what you paid for. You get to satisfy yourself that I am what I said... you know... a virgin."

*Oh fuck.*

"There's no need for…"

"I want to. Please? I want to show you what a good girl I've been, saving myself for you. Please, D-" She paused. "Kris."

It was the hottest thing I'd ever heard come out of a girl's mouth. The way she said it, sounding younger and more inexperienced than even *she* was, yet so desperate to be a good girl for me was too much to resist. I had to see what she wanted to show.

I cupped her ass with both hands and lifted her off the ground. She wrapped her legs around me and, *finally*, I felt my hard cock nuzzling up against her panty-clad pussy as I carried her to her room.

Nudging the door open with my foot, while we kissed, we entered and I climbed on to the bed on my knees with Amy still wrapped around me. I leaned over and she let go so her weight fell on the mattress.

Amy scooted slowly backwards away from me, taking deep breaths as if she was having to concentrate on every one of them. When her back hit the pillows, she stopped for a second and then reached for the hem of her dress with shaking hands.

Inch by inch, she pulled her dress up. If she was a more experienced girl, I would have said she was doing it to tease me, a practiced and sultry act. With Amy, though, it was pure nerves. She couldn't do it any faster if she tried.

Her eyes were on me, rather than on what she was doing. Her panic was held in check only by her excitement, and I read a million pleas in her expression.

*I can't believe this is happening…*
*Please like me…*

I remembered my own first time getting naked, with a more experienced girl, over two decades ago. I remembered how all the bravado, the whole act, became useless as I was literally laid bare before her. She would either like what she saw, or crush me. Now that power over Amy was *mine*.

When her dress was bunched up around her hips, I tore my eyes away from hers and looked down to see she was actually still wearing her bikini bottoms from earlier. Amy glanced down, then back at me.

"You can untie them," she said, her voice wavering.

At each hip, the bikini bottoms were tied in bow. I reached for one, grasping the string between my finger and thumb and tugged at it. The knot came undone and the string went loose on that side. I did the same with the other knot.

Amy's hand snapped down between her legs, holding the tiny scrap of black material against her, and her legs closed too. In her eyes, the panic seemed to have won a battle in the war against excitement.

She was breathing heavily, as if recovering from a short run and preparing for another. Her eyes started to get a glassy look.

"I'm sorry," she said. "I want to… I want this… to be good… um…"

"Shhhh. You can't help but be perfect. Show me what's mine."

I placed my hands on her knees and worked my fingers between her legs. With slowly increasing pressure, I pushed them away from each other until she relaxed and they started moving.

Once her legs were parted, I carefully grasped her hand at the wrist and pulled it away from her bikini bottoms. Now there was almost nothing between me and her virgin pussy.

I pinched the flimsy material at the top and pulled it down, revealing Amy had not the faintest hint of even a narrow landing strip, she'd been waxed bare. Then I laid eyes on her untouched slit for the first time. For that matter, it was the first time I'd had *any* virgin girl's legs spread before me. Every woman I'd been with had been around the block once or twice.

In that moment, I would have believed that not even Amy's own finger had been inside of her, her pussy looked so tight. There was no doubt in my mind she was exactly what she'd been advertised as.

Yet, I knew this brief glance wasn't what the terms and conditions meant by 'inspection.' There was better evidence of her innocence to be had. The only question was would I be able to hold myself back?

# Chapter 11

## Amy

Everything Ada told me to say, everything that men wanted to hear, was all out the window in this moment. I was totally exposed and vulnerable in front of this vastly more experienced man.

My clothes were gone, my legs were parted, his eyes were fixed on my sex. I could feel I was a little wet, from the excitement of the car ride back home and the thrill of him carrying me to the bedroom with that huge bulge of his nestled against me.

That slickness was a remnant of recent times when I had something to hide behind. Those days were gone, and I had no idea if the evidence of how turned on I'd been was plain for him to see or not.

If it was, then my vulnerability was absolute. He'd be able to see how much I wanted him, but I had no idea how to read that expression on his face now that he'd seen what he bought.

Did I look... *weird* down there? Did he hate the scars on my thigh? Some part of me accused the rest of overthinking this, that I should remember this was just business. It was a dangerous thing, to let my guard down, to run the risk of having actual *feelings* for a man more than twice my age who had bought my virginity.

That was easier said than done, though. He was *magnetic*, everything he did he *mastered*. I was drawn to him much more than I should have been. On one hand, it made *this* infinitely easier than the horror-stories I'd been imagining since the close of my auction. On the other hand, there was that danger of setting myself up for an embarrassing heartbreak, and other things that were even worse.

I'd been *this close* to messing up in the living room, to letting out my own deepest darkest fantasies. My attraction to him had put me too much at ease, but he'd have sent me packing if I'd done that.

"You are so *fucking* sexy, Amy," he breathed.

I let out a breath I didn't know I'd been holding and my legs relaxed, parting even further than before. Kris pulled at my bikini bottoms and the material slid out from under my ass. He tossed them aside without looking where they were going.

A moment later, his jacket was flying across the room too. The way he filled his shirt, the material straining at his chest and biceps, made me squirm involuntarily in anticipation despite my nerves.

Kris lifted my right foot and placed it on his left shoulder, then slowly stroked the skin of my inner leg from ankle to mid-thigh, where my scars were. Everywhere he touched he left a trail of faint pins and needles that made my breath catch in my throat.

Turning his head, he kissed my ankle and I pointed my toes in response. With slow purpose, he kissed his way along the inside of my calf, and I watched, mesmerized.

Every touch of his lips made me want to whimper blissfully. It took a supreme effort of willpower to stop those sounds from escaping as I watched him treat my leg like it was priceless.

He raised my foot so he could kiss the back of my knee and the surprise spike of pleasure was too much for me. My hands flung to the covers and gripped twin fistfuls, as the sensation of an itch being scratched hummed from the back of my leg to my clit and back again.

"Oooh!" I squealed.

Kris smirked and tortured me with licks and sucks to the back of my knee until I was right on the borderline of having to pull away from him. Just when I thought I couldn't handle it anymore, he resumed his journey up my leg, kissing my inner thigh just above the knee.

I calmed down from the sweet surprise of how much I liked getting kisses to the back of the knee, and grew quiet when he came to the scars. If I had to bet, I would have expected him to pass over them and continue closer to my pussy.

If I had done that, I would have lost my wager. I bit my lip when he kissed my scars as if they were invisible, then continued upwards.

The higher he went, the more sensitive my skin became, and I was acutely aware of the stubble that framed every one of his kisses. Its rough texture tantalized me, and now that he was close enough, I reached down to stroke his cheek as he closed in on my most closely guarded treasure.

Finally, I felt his lips on my skin right next to my labia. It couldn't really be classified as leg anymore, he was that close.

I felt his hot breath puff out on my entrance, cooling the natural lubricants that were slowly seeping out, and a moment later I felt a man's tongue on my sex for the very first time in my life. My eyes closed and my head lolled back as I moaned in bliss.

I was in no position to judge whether it *always* felt so good to have a guy go down on you, or if Kris was simply an expert at it, but either way, *this* was the life. He licked the full length of my pussy, slowly and purposefully on each side before his tongue slid into my slit to sample my flowing nectar.

He tasted me once and then again, a deeper lick that ended with a gentle flick across my clit. The sudden shock of pleasure made me yelp, then run my fingers through his hair.

Kris alternated between licking, kissing and sucking my folds, the prickles from his stubble merging with the tingling sensation his lips and tongue elicited. I could feel that delicious roughness on my inner thighs when my legs twitched together and hugged his face.

Between his licks and my ever-increasing arousal, my pussy felt wetter than ever before. The wetter I became, the faster he licked. It was a wonderful upward spiral of pleasure.

"Woooow," I moaned, like some hippie on a psychedelic trip.

Kris turned his attentions to my clit and my head snapped up so I could watch what was happening between my legs. I gripped and released the covers several times, then my hands seemed to move of their own accord without any clear plan as to what was the best course of action.

I grabbed the headboard, ran my hands through both mine and his hair, squeezed my breasts through my dress, stroked his cheek and even reached as far as caressing one of his biceps through his shirt, all within the space of a few minutes.

His lips were latched on to me and his tongue flicked back and forth across my most sensitive spot at a furious pace. An electric buzz was running from my clit to my stomach where it was collecting like a ball of lightning, threatening to strike me down if it grew big enough.

My hips began to buck, to instinctively grind against his face, as that threat came close to realization. My eyelids closed halfway and I started panting, my voice catching with every exhalation and forcing louder and louder moans out of me.

Just when my toes curled in preparation for my first orgasm, Kris pulled back, and the only thing touching my clit was his breath. My eyes rolled back down from up in my head and I blinked until my vision cleared.

"What… what are you doing?" I couldn't keep the edge of desperation out of my voice.

He didn't say anything, just gave me an all-knowing smirk, and bent his head down again, kissing next to my pussy on each side, licking up any errant juices that had escaped beyond the realm of my most intimate parts, but being careful not to touch anything that might push me over the edge until my climax had receded back into the shadows.

Then he started all over again. The slow licks along the full length of my folds, finishing with a sustained assault on my clit that drove me crazy.

Despite his best efforts, enough slippery juices escaped so that I could feel a wet patch under my ass. I was too far gone to care, all I cared about was the sweet release he was teasing me with.

The muscles of my stomach were taut with the strain of containing that humming mass of electric ecstasy. My humility was blown out of the water and he had me moaning with complete abandon as he brought me to the brink a second time... and once again left me hanging.

I was almost crying with need. The tears were welling up and if I blinked hard enough they would squeeze out and flow down my cheeks. How could something that felt so good be so torturous?

"*Please...*" I put every ounce of need I could into my voice.

Kris started the cycle again, and I gripped the headboard with all my strength as my strained muscles bordered on the verge of cramping. This time, when his tongue was whirling over my clit, I felt his finger circling my entrance for a while, getting good and slippery.

After a few minutes, he slipped it inside me, just barely to the first knuckle, and my pussy hugged it tight. I felt him gently pushing at my hymen. He had his evidence.

*Oh my gosh, there's a man inside me!*

It wasn't his big dick, but there was no denying that my entrance was gripping his finger on all sides, and my entire being was aware of it. I could feel it inside me on the sensitive untouched walls of my vagina. Kris was inside of me in a way totally different to how the tip of his tongue had touched mine when we kissed.

Not only that, this time he didn't stop his magic tongue on my clit and the ball of lightning zapped me, making all my muscles flex even tighter, making me twitch with undignified euphoria. My heartbeat was the reverberating clap of thunder in my ears, drowning out all other sounds.

If my moans were coming in the form of coherent words, I couldn't hear them. My lips were numb, so there were no clues there about what I might have been saying, if it wasn't gibberish.

After a while, the sound of my heartbeat receded and I could hear myself panting. The ball lightning in my stomach was still there, but smaller, floating around a wide-open space that it used to fill completely, as if searching for an exit.

I looked down and saw Kris standing at the foot of the bed, framed on either side, from my perspective, by my quivering knees. Blinking again to clear my vision, I smiled at him dazedly.

"I've got to go, see you in the morning," he said.

My brow knitted together and my smile disappeared in the confusion. "Wha?"

He didn't offer any explanation to my highly pertinent question. He just left, and closed the door behind him. I might have followed him to repeat it if I had any confidence that my legs might have supported my weight at that moment.

# Chapter 12

# Kris

That was a close call, and it had only been the second day. I couldn't have had a worse sleep if my mattress had been stuffed with a German Oom-pah band practicing for Oktoberfest.

I usually slept on my stomach, but I couldn't this time because my permanently hard dick made it too uncomfortable. Thoughts of Amy's perfect little pussy haunted me, and when I was lying on my back, every twitch of the covers against my erection made me think of how incredible it would feel to have the head of my cock pushing into her, breaking through that hymen and going balls-deep.

Eventually I had to throw the covers off and fall into a fitful sleep on my back. If the maid had come in early, she would have got an eyeful. Maybe she would have worked for free from then on, or maybe I would have had to explain that I was actually doing an impression of a sundial and this was not grounds to have me charged with sexual harassment.

Thankfully, I woke up from my broken sleep to my alarm, and a trip to the gym followed by an interrogation-level cold shower had me more or less ready to face Amy again. Once more, I heard her shower going while I ate breakfast. I turned to face her when she emerged wearing the bathrobe again.

In that moment I wondered if this week was going to kill me. The last time I'd seen her, she'd been spread-eagled on the bed with a wet pussy and quivering legs, hair all messed up from thrashing her head back and forth. If I managed to resist a sight like that a couple more times, then I had a strong case to go to the pope and seek out sainthood.

Yet, as incredible as that had been, she looked even better like this. Mostly covered, yet vulnerable. I wanted to unwrap her like a present over and over again. Every time I unwrapped her would be like seeing her naked for the first time, I was sure of it. Her body spoke to mine in ways I never dreamed were possible.

It took a little reassuring to let her know that everything was OK. The fact that we still had plenty of time to go, and even the most socially inept person could see I was wildly attracted to her, probably helped my case. What would I do as the days were crossed off the week though? How could I deflect her advances and not lose my mind?

She was right when she said I was keeping us busy. The least amount of time we spent together alone in this penthouse, the better. I had to keep us out there, make every situation as unsuitable for fucking as I could, without outright treating her like shit.

Today, it was Obvius.ly to the rescue. We were spending the whole day doing shit, and hopefully by the end of it she'd be so exhausted and we'd be so sick of each other that it wouldn't take much to convince her that we could wait at least another day before getting intimate.

First on the agenda was an Italian cooking class. Amy clapped and bounced gleefully when I told her, and snuggled up in the car on the way, talking excitedly about what she hoped to make.

I slipped my arm around her as we talked and she just... *fit* against me. It felt right, somehow. There was something I couldn't put my finger on. It was more than her physical perfection, I was sure of that much.

I'd been with more girls than I could count, but none of them felt like this. Although I never paid for sex before, Amy looked at me with more natural affection in her eyes than any of the others from the more natural encounters I'd had with women.

It was difficult to reconcile that sense with the amount of money it actually took to *put* Amy by my side. She was either the greatest actress the world had ever known, or she was just as sweet as she seemed.

If I thought getting her in an apron and a chef's hat would downplay her sex appeal, I was wrong. She spent half the time during our class with a smudge of flour on the tip of her nose that was downright adorable.

She let me wipe it off for her, scrunching up her nose a little, before the instructor cooked the pizzas and ravioli we'd made. We washed up and sat in the restaurant the instructor ran from the same space, waiting for lunch.

"Oh my gosh, I'm so hungry!" she said.

"Whose pizza do you think is going to be the best?" I asked.

She waved her hand dismissively. "Pfff. Please. It's going to be mine."

I laughed. "How can you be so sure? I've got ten different kinds of meat on mine!"

"That's pushing it! There weren't even ten different kinds of animal to choose from," she said.

"Yeah... but ham is not bacon. Peperoni is not ground beef."

"Yeah, yeah. Ham cut into circles is not ham cut into triangles is not ham cut into parallelograms..." she teased with a smile.

My eyes narrowed playfully. "Hmmm... this sounds personal."

"How so?"

"Well, you said you lived on a farm. Do you think there's something on my pizza that you might have raised? Am I going to be eating an old friend?"

"I don't know. It's a wheat farm, so you can understand it's difficult for me to keep track of every grain of flour, but... some of it did look kind of familiar." Melodramatic horror dawned on her face. "You don't think... it couldn't be... Captain Wheatface? He always kissed me on the nose! Nooo!"

I cracked up at the pet name. "My parents got me a dog to teach me responsibility, I guess your mom was a bit more conservative."

"I guess so. One day I might work my way up to a fish."

"Let's not get ahead of ourselves. Who's running the farm while you're away?"

"Oh, we don't run it ourselves. My mom's leased it out since before I can remember. The only thing I grow there myself is a whole bunch of aloe vera, and I didn't see any of that in the kitchen." She jerked a thumb in the direction of the door.

"Aloe vera, huh? What do you do with it?"

"Nothing really... it just grows."

I frowned, trying to understand. "How much is 'a bunch'?"

"I've got a greenhouse jam-packed with it. Like, twenty yards long by ten yards wide, four tiers in each row."

I held my hands in claw-shapes at each of my temples, then moved them out, extending my fingers and making an explosion sound. "Mind: Blown. You've got to explain."

Amy pulled her hands off the table and fidgeted with them in her lap for a while. Her eyes flickered up at me, then back down.

"Um... It's hard to... well... you know how I told you my mom's in a wheelchair?"

"Yeah."

"It's because she and my dad were in a car accident when I was only one. A *bad* car accident. He died and she never walked again."

"Oh. Oh, Amy, I'm sorry."

She shook her head. "It's before I could remember anyway."

I tried to think about what my first memory was. I had a vision of looking down at my foot and seeing stitches coming out of the side of my toe. My parents told me I needed stitches when a footstool broke under me while I was using it to reach a light switch when I was two and a half.

"You weren't in the car, were you?" I asked, thinking of the scars on her thigh.

"No, my aunt was babysitting me that night."

"OK."

"So, apparently, my dad used to grow orchids as a kind of hobby. That's why we had the greenhouse, but by the time my mom returned to the farm, you know, things had kind of gone to hell. All the orchids were dead, but my dad's aloe vera plant was still fighting the good fight. It used to belong to his grandmother, so my mom was glad it survived. She took care of it for a little bit, but as soon as I was big enough to water it, she gave officially gave it to me. It's been in my family for four generations!"

"That's amazing, how long do they live for?"

"I really don't know, it just keeps on going."

"Where did the rest of them come from then?"

"From the first one. New plants sprouted up around the big one non-stop, it seemed. By the time I was five, the pot it was in was full of aloe vera plants of various sizes. I tracked down every kind of container I could and my mom showed me how to transplant the little ones."

"Oh... then they grew and sprouted even more new plants..."

"And so on. Eventually I had to scavenge all over the neighborhood to get enough pots for them all to grow in. It's always just been my *thing*. My way of staying connected to my dad. Something I was able to do from a really early age. It felt like I took what he left me and made it flourish. You know?" she said.

"I know *exactly* what you mean. My dad busted his balls to get me my education, and my parents loaned me some money when I needed it, while I was waiting for an idea to pay off. To take all their self-sacrifice and make something... amazing out of it has always been something that's driven me."

Amy breathed a sigh of relief and reached out across the table to hold my hand.

"Actually, you remember how you were saying the other day you wish you had a business idea?" I prompted.

"You mean I should sell the plants? I don't know if I could do that. Who would buy them from me anyway, when they can get them at the local Home Depot?"

"The Home Depot is a faceless giant corporation. You've got a *story*. And a face, a really pretty one. If you get a space at the local farmer's market, print up something that tells the story, I bet they'd fly off the shelves. A very special plant that's been in your family for four generations, your father's legacy to you. People would love it."

"But..."

"And if it works, you can make space for more plants. Make what he left you flourish even further."

"Hmmm." She seemed to be mulling it over.

"I don't know how fast they grow so you could replace your stock, or how much they go for, but it's worth looking at the numbers."

Amy's smile reached her eyes. "OK, I'll do that. Thanks!"

The door to the kitchen bumped open and our teacher-turned-waiter came through backwards, carrying a tray with our food on it. She spun around and came our way.

"Lunch is served!"

# Chapter 13

# Amy

I didn't know what to expect when I opened the bedroom door in the morning. My mind went to some reasonably dark places when Kris left after giving me the most explosive orgasm of my life. Had I said something weird in my climactic delirium? Did my face contort into some grotesque shape when I came?

I had no way of knowing. What I *did* know, was that the man at the breakfast bar who turned to face me, knew my body more intimately than any other man on the planet.

He had spread my legs, taken off my underwear, and blown my mind. He had touched what no man ever had. It gave him a kind of power over me, as if he needed any more.

I *knew* he was attracted to me, if the bulge he had in his pants when he left was anything to go by. But he still left. What was I doing wrong?

He assured me it was nothing and then we had the most incredible date ever. We made our own lunch under the guidance of a real Italian cook, and then I found myself opening up to him more than Ada had recommended.

She said not to break the illusion that the perfect sex partner had been delivered to him, but I didn't quite know how to get around the questions he asked. Besides, there was something about how he knew me so intimately already that made me want to share more with him. Even some of the bad stuff.

So I did, and it felt great. He didn't even think I was the aloe vera equivalent of a crazy cat lady. Maybe it *was* worth considering if I could sell some of my plants.

I drew a little cartoon picture of us on the back of a paper napkin and gave it to him before we left, and he said I had a nice style.

After lunch, we went ice skating, and I never saw anything so funny in my life. Our town actually had an ice skating rink, so I'd been a few times, but it was something Kris had never done before.

He looked about as graceful as a newborn giraffe, and I had to skate backwards holding his hands to keep him upright for longer than five seconds at a time. Even then he still managed to fall over in spectacular fashion.

"You gotta push from side to side a bit, not straight forward-"

"Do I *look* Canadian to you?" he said from flat on his back on the ice. "Speak *English*!"

It was too funny, I doubled over laughing and ended up on my knees next to him. Together, we managed to get up again. It was a temporary thing for him, but we made our way around the rink a few times and had a blast.

Then the tables turned when we went to an indoor rock-climbing place. The person who met us there seemed surprised to see only two of us, because apparently Kris had to book for fifty people in order for them to close and let us have the whole venue to ourselves.

I'd never been great at handling heights, so I wasn't looking forward to this. It *looked* fun, and the automatic belay system brought me gently down when I tested it from a yard or two off the ground, but the thought of going *all the way up there* was terrifying.

In addition to standard rock-climbing walls, they had a bunch of themed walls of various difficulties, including a big one that was done in an Indiana Jones style treasure-hunting adventure. The wall had little rope ladders strung over crocodile infested rivers painted on the surface, temples, caves, something that looked like a bullwhip to swing across on, and a bunch of other things that were difficult to see in detail because they were so high off the ground and the angle was so acute.

At the top was the ancient treasure we were supposed to aim for. I swore there were clouds partially obscuring the upper reaches of this wall.

"I don't think I can do this," I said.

"I'll stay with you the whole way," said Kris, clipping the safety rope on to his harness. "If it'll make it easier for you, you can put on some ice skates."

I rolled my eyes with a half-smile, but clipped myself on and took my spot at the bottom of the wall at one side, while Kris went to my right. It was bearable for the first several sets of hand and footholds, but then I made the mistake of looking down.

If I fell from here, I was sure I'd survive, but if I fell awkwardly it was high enough to break something. Immediately, I clung close to the wall for dear life.

Kris made his way over to me and put his hand on my back. "It's OK, you've got this. Remember, you've got the safety rope, nothing bad can happen."

*Yeah right, unless I twist around and crack my skull on the wall or the safety rope snaps.*

"Right," I said.

With him pointing out nearly every hand and foothold I should take, we scaled our way upward over the course of a century or two. My hands were almost cramped up from gripping the handholds so tightly when I looked down again.

Falling from this height was certain death, and I tried to melt into the wall entirely. Sweat was pouring off my brow and the palms of my hands were slippery with it, compounding my problems.

Yet, we were only one rickety bridge away from the golden skull sitting on top of a pedestal. Kris went part of the way across and held his hand back to me.

My eyes darted from his hand to mine and back again as if they were inconceivably far apart. Then, taking a few deep breaths to work up the nerve, I made a mad grab for it, almost losing my footing in the process.

With a thundering heart and squeezing Kris' hand almost hard enough to break it, I shuffled across the bridge and joined him on the other side. There was a little button on top of the golden skull.

Kris took my hand, which he was still holding, and we pressed the button together. A light at the top of the wall started flashing and the sound of a crowd cheering played from some speakers.

My ordeal wasn't over though, since I was stranded halfway to space up here.

"OK, just grab on to the rope, lean back and let it take you down."

I shook my head furiously in a panic. "I can't!"

"Uh… alright, just try this for a start, OK? Hold on to my arm with both hands. I've got a good grip with the other hand, see? I *will not* let you go. I promise. Do you believe me?"

My eyes started slipping towards the ground again.

"Hey, do you believe me?"

I looked up at him and nodded.

"Good. Once you're happy with your grip, and I'll hold on to you too, I'll lean you out just a little bit so you can see what it feels like, alright?"

I nodded again and quickly transferred my other hand from the wall to his arm when he was ready. Slowly, with my feet planted at the base of the pedestal, he extended his arm to make me lean out.

Instead of looking down, I concentrated on the way his bicep strained at the hole of his sleeve and managed to lose myself in my own little world for a few seconds. When his arm was fully extended, he started straightening his other one, the one holding the wall.

"How's that?" he asked.

"It's OK," I said.

"You comfortable?"

"Sort of."

"OK, here we go."

Before I could say a single word, he let go with his hand gripping the wall and we started floating towards the ground together. I screamed and squeezed my eyes shut.

When I didn't feel the impact of my body on the ground, followed by broken bones and squished internal organs, I opened my eyes again. The automatic belay system, attached to the safety rope, controlled the rate of decent.

It was a slow pace, a difficult pace to be terrified by. I looked up at Kris' smiling face.

"Told you I wouldn't let you go."

"OK, you got me. This is actually pretty cool."

My feet touched the ground and I felt exhilaration flow through me far beyond what the flashing light and canned cheering had done. I stumbled a little as I took my own weight, but recovered and reattached the safety rope to the anchor on the ground so it didn't retract itself to the top of the wall.

Once that was done, I bounded over to Kris and leapt up to wrap my arms around his neck, my feet dangling off the ground. His arms circled around me and I tilted my head to the side as he kissed me.

In my post-adrenaline state, I was sweaty, I was shaking, it was probably the *least* well-groomed I'd looked since arriving at the airport, but the way Kris kissed me made me feel like I'd just been crowned as a beauty queen. He was proud to be with me, proud *of* me.

We'd had the pecks on the cheek, we'd had the can't-get-enough-of-you deep kisses in the car, there was something different about this one. This felt real. More real than any kiss I'd had from previous boyfriends.

There was no sense that he felt like he'd paid me to be here, and the kiss was so wonderful that I forgot it myself. It was so sweet that I curled one leg up behind me as I relished the feel of our lips dancing with one another. I couldn't help it.

# Chapter 14

# Kris

Girls from the clubs never kissed like that. In fact, *I'd* never kissed a girl like that. As much as I wanted Amy, as excited as she was about surviving her ordeal, it was a slow kiss. It was a kiss where I could appreciate every movement of her lips against mine, and it made me want more.

Luckily for me, after the indoor rock-climbing, I'd arranged for a personal shopper to take Amy out so she could buy anything she wanted to get ready for dinner tonight. Amy seemed kind of bewildered by the idea, but went with it.

She was downright apologetic when she arrived in the evening. I'd told the personal shopper to take her to the high-end stores, but Amy had desperately tried to find the least expensive things she could. To spend over thirty thousand dollars on a single outfit's worth of clothes and jewelry was clearly alien to her.

Despite coming in so far under the budget I'd given, she wore it well. The earrings complimented her own necklace, the dress showed off her slim shape and the thin gold bracelet added a nice flash of color to the ensemble.

I arrived before her at the restaurant and it made me feel like a king when she arrived. To see every head in the room turning and knowing that she was coming to *my* table was unreal.

By the time dinner was over and we were on our way back home, I'd spent almost all the time I was required to spend with Amy. It had been a long and active day, and the mood in the car on the way back was more relaxed than ever.

However, when we arrived back and the door shut behind us, I discovered it wasn't relaxed enough. Amy had been cuddling up quietly in the car and I hoped she might want to go straight to sleep now, but she gave me a big hug instead.

"I had an incredible day with you," she said.

"Me too."

"I think we should make it even more incredible."

"I don't know… I was thinking of getting an early night. Aren't you tired?"

"Nope."

Amy steered us in the direction of the couch and I sank down when it hit me in the back of the knees. She stood between my legs and turned around before sitting, with her ass right against my crotch.

With a shy look over her shoulder, she pulled her golden hair out of the way. "Could you unzip me?"

My hands moved of their own accord. I should have stalled, I should have thought about the millions of dollars and the smug look on Kevin's face, but I *had* to see her body.

I grasped the top of her dress with one hand and pulled the zip down with the other. As the material parted, I saw the black strap of a bra across her back, and the top of a matching pair of panties at the bottom of the zip.

"Thanks," she said, standing again.

Still facing away, Amy shrugged the dress off her shoulders. Holding it against her chest, she turned to face me.

"Mary made me buy a set of underwear too. Sorry again."

I waved the notion away. "I said it's fine. I expected you to spend more."

"I guess a lot of girls come after you for your money, huh?"

"It's... been known to happen."

"Well... I know this might be difficult to believe, given how we met and all, but I'm really not like them. I need the money, but I like you too, Kris. I'm glad it was you waiting for me at the airport on Sunday and not somebody else. I was so scared, but now... I want you to see me."

She let her dress fall slowly, more due to nerves than any innate knowledge about how fucking sexy it was. The gentle curves of her small breasts cupped in her bra were revealed, and then her flat stomach.

"I like it when you touch me," she continued.

Her dress fell to her upper thighs, and I could only barely make out the faint outline of her labia where her new panties hugged her. She let go of the dress completely and it pooled on the floor around her before she stepped out of it and flicked it to the side with one foot.

"I'm sorry if that all sounds stupid, I don't know how to be... sexy, like the other girls. I *do* know that I want to make you feel good."

Amy sank to her knees on the floor in front of me and rested her hands on my thighs. She licked her lips and gulped.

I was as still as a statue, worried that if I made any move at all, my instincts would have me tearing off her last scraps of clothes and fucking her to within an inch of her life. These were dangerous waters.

No. Dangerous wasn't a strong enough word to describe sailing through enemy territory in a sea that had more mines than water. I was on a hair trigger at this point, and this little teen who had no idea how sexy she was could probably make me cum harder than I had in my entire life.

Her hand moved up my thigh and caressed my hardening cock. She gasped and I held my breath for a second.

She looked up at me, then back down at what she was doing, unbuttoning my pants, then grabbing my zipper and doing for me what I'd done for her. Amy grasped my pants and underwear all at once, and when her pretty blue eyes flicked up again, I knew what she needed.

I lifted my weight off the couch and she tugged my pants and boxers down. My semi-hard cock twitched a little as it was unveiled by the receding clothing. Amy's eyes widened.

Her jaw dropped slightly, parting her lips, and her eyes scanned up and down its length, but she was otherwise still. Her chest swelled as she took a deep breath.

"Wow."

# Chapter 15

# Amy

His cock was like nothing I'd ever seen before. It didn't seem right putting it in the same category of 'thing' as Anthony's. Anthony had a slingshot, Kris had an intercontinental ballistic missile.

It was terrifying and entrancing all at once. I felt like an engineer flying an experimental paper plane into Kris' airspace, marveling at the technical brilliance of the weapons of war flying at me.

A cock like that could destroy a petite girl like me, but it was so incredibly magnificent that I couldn't think of a better way to go out. I wanted to touch it, to see how much I could endure.

I tentatively wrapped both of my hands around it and felt its weight. It throbbed against my palms and I could feel my grip getting forced wider as it hardened.

"You like that?" he asked.

I nodded. It was hypnotic.

I shuffled forward until my knees were touching the front of the couch. Kris' cock was supporting its own weight now, standing up straight and hard, my hands were just along for the ride.

Bending down, I gave the head of his cock a tender kiss with trembling lips. It swelled in my hands, becoming iron-hard for a moment. I kissed it repeatedly, worshipping it on all sides, and felt it respond to my touch each time.

Cocking my elbows out, I made room for a kissing-exploration along the underside of his shaft, using both hands to pull his hard length towards me. At the pace I was going, it took an eternity to traverse the length of his manhood and reach his balls.

I stuck my tongue out and found one, licking it upwards then letting it fall back down, before kissing it and repeating on the other one. Kris groaned and let his head roll back on the couch so he was looking up at the ceiling.

Taking it as a good sign, I paid careful attention to his balls for a couple minutes before working my way back up his shaft. I kept my eyes on the tip of his cock all the way, intimidated by its thickness, its incredible length.

What would it be like to take that inside me? I mean, this wasn't merely his tongue, or his finger. Aside from the sheer size, this was the core of his physical sexuality.

After that cock had been inside me, it was official. My virginity would be gone, it would belong to him forever. They say you never forget your first.

I arrived at the tip of his cock and, after one last timid kiss, I let my tongue circle around it. Kris raised his head to watch me and I turned my eyes up to him, trying to read if I was doing this to his satisfaction or not.

Physically, he was leaned way back in the couch. In his eyes, he was on the edge of his seat. The fire burning there flared with every swirl of my tongue and I felt a surge of power in response.

This wealthy, experienced, sexy as hell older man was hanging on my every movement. I paused the swirling of my tongue and feinted at taking him into my mouth, and he stopped breathing, only to resume when my tongue ran another lap around the tip.

I smiled, as much as I could with my tongue sticking out, and wondered if my expression was anything like his all-knowing smirk. Pausing again, with the head of his cock resting on my tongue, our eyes locked and I opened wide to slide him past my lips.

Ada gave me a crash-course in blowjob basics, even had me practice on a dildo, but it was all academic. It paled in comparison to dealing with the reality of having a thick cock in my mouth, a masculine invader.

Kris reached over my shoulder, behind my back and I heard the snap of his fingers as my bra came loose. He gathered up my hair into a single ponytail, gripped in one hand, as I let go of his manhood to shrug my bra off.

Using his grip, he wrestled control of the situation away from me and moved my head up and down to bob on his cock as I threw my bra away. I rested my hands on his thighs again, even pulled them in a little so my nipples brushed against them as he moved me.

I moaned right on his cock as my sensitive pink tips rubbed on his legs, and Kris caught his breath, holding my head dead still as his cock swelled in my mouth. My eyes widened and I froze too, thinking I was going to taste a man's cum for the first time.

It didn't happen.  After walking a proverbial razor's edge for an eternity, he pulled my head off his cock, and with his hands in my hair he brought both of us to our feet.  Kris wrapped one arm around my waist and held me tightly against him, while his other hand went down the front of my panties and one finger slid between my folds.

Conflicting instincts of modesty and need nearly tore me apart.  The ease with which his finger slipped between my legs, aided by my undeniable wetness, was proof I'd meant what I said about wanting him to touch me.  At the same time, the idea of a man having access to the most carefully guarded parts of my body was impossible to get used to.

My legs tried to open to give him easier access, and close to guard my virgin entrance, all at the same time, and ended up doing nothing except going weak at the knees when his finger rubbed my slippery juices all over my clit.  I leaned back, whimpering in pleasure, and my chest thrust out at Kris.  He took the opportunity to lean way down and take a nipple into his mouth, sending a spark of electric pleasure tingling into my body.

With much of my weight supported by Kris, I pushed my underwear down and unbuttoned his shirt with hands shaking from the pure bliss he was forcing me to experience.  Every movement of his finger against my clit was making me slicker by the second, and I could hear the wet sounds with each flick.

Kris disentangled himself from the pants around his ankles and brought us back down to the couch.  He turned to the side and laid himself down on his back, with me sitting on the edge.

I was trembling with nerves about what was about to happen. But just as I was about to move to straddle him, he pulled at my thigh, spinning me around so that my knees were on either side of his head with my pussy hovering over his mouth, and I was facing his feet.

He pulled my ass down and his mouth made contact with my pussy, that magic tongue of his flicking from side to side across my clit. I gasped and flopped forward, bracing myself with my hands on either side of his hips.

His cock twitched and throbbed right in front of me, with pre-cum and my own saliva smeared all over the head. With me being so short, but his cock being so long, it was perfectly positioned for me to slip it into my mouth again.

Kris was eating my pussy not only like there was no tomorrow, but like there might be no next *minute*. It was a blur of intense sensations between my legs, quickly building up like my climax the previous night while his hands squeezed my ass *hard*, making sure there was no escape.

I tried to concentrate on making him feel as good as he was making *me* feel, but if it was a competition, I was no match for his experience. He knew *exactly* what to do, whereas I was on the verge of forgetting my own name.

My orgasm built and built until all I could do was grip his cock hard with my hand, and moan on it while multi-colored lights burst in front of my eyes, forcing me to squeeze them shut. My legs quivered in climactic ecstasy on either side of his head as his tongue relentlessly forced every last scrap of pleasure possible out of my body.

Finally, after what might have been close to forever, the pleasure that had tickled me from head to toe receded. At least with a mouthful of cock I wasn't worried about having said something stupid, and I pulled back, letting it pop out of my mouth.

I shuffled forward and turned around, moving to kneel between his legs as Kris sat up. My hair felt like it had gone wild, *I* felt like I had gone wild. I reached out to caress his inked abs, feeling like I wanted to lick, bite, kiss and scratch him all at once.

Panting like I'd never catch my breath, I leaned back until my head was on the armrest and Kris was following me, about to move over me. He paused.

"Goodnight, Amy," he said with a strained voice.

"Huh?"

Kris stood, his dick as hard as a rock and without stopping to collect his clothes, headed in the direction of his room. I struggled to sit up.

"Are you serious?" I asked his retreating back.

"See you in the morning," he said.

What the hell was going on?

# Chapter 16

# Kris

Amy looked crestfallen in the morning, on the verge of asking a million questions, but she was much quieter than normal. It dampened any minor sense of triumph I had left about being able to pull back from *that* close. My balls aching for release all night had taken care of the rest of that triumph already.

I hated having put that look on her face. Best case scenario would be that she had given up and wouldn't try so hard anymore. I hated even more that this was supposed to be a win under the circumstances.

This was a fucked up idea. I never would have taken the bet if I had known what Amy would be like beforehand. Cute, sexy, fun to spend time with, she was so young and full of potential that she was exhilarating to be around.

She even had some talent as an artist, if the little cartoon she made on the napkin was anything to go by. Seeing it gave me an idea that was potentially going to be a life-saver for me today.

I had several hopeful entrepreneurs lined up who were going to be pitching me their business ideas this morning at the Obvius.ly offices, looking for investment. Originally, I was going to let Amy do her own thing and meet up after lunch, but that meant I was going to have to spend a lot more time with her in the evening. Dangerous.

Instead, I brought her in with me. Several times in the past, during team meetings, when we had a lot of brainstorming going on or people were spit-balling whatever, it had proven incredibly useful to have an artist drawing up the ideas as quickly as they could.

Sometimes *seeing* an idea like that made all the difference. It was a technique I'd borrowed from a friend of mine who worked in the film industry. They often brought some talented writers into a room together to talk about ideas for a particular movie property, be it some old cartoon show from the 80s or the latest superhero character, as the writers talked, the artists drew what they talked about. Some incredible visuals came out of that, and it worked for me too.

Now Amy was set up in the corner of the boardroom with everything she could possibly hope for from a sketch-artist perspective. She could spend the entire morning doing what she loved in a professional setting, and save me the hours of temptation later.

"Pre-cum doesn't count, right?"

"Huh?" said Kevin.

"Pre-cum. She started giving me a blowjob," I said.

"But didn't *finish*?"

"No. Fuck you, by the way."

Kevin laughed. "It's the beginning of the end. I ain't worried, I don't need a pity win. OK, pre-cum doesn't count. How many you got scheduled for this morning?"

"Five."

"Pick us a winner. What's Amy doing here?"

"Getting her to sketch the pitches and I'm spending quality time with her, of course," I said.

"She's an artist?"

"Aspiring. She's pretty good from what little I've seen too, so thought it might be worth trying the technique for pitches while she's around, you know?"

"Couldn't hurt, interesting idea. Hey, I spoke to Anson last night. He said he'd be calling us sometime today with some news. Reading between the lines... I think it sounds good. You might need to cut a pitch short to get in on the phone call."

I sucked in some air through pursed lips. "Holy fuck... this could be it, man."

"Finally, we'll be able to make ends meet," Kevin laughed.

"The wolf will have to find somebody else's door. Alright, catch up with you later."

I headed back to the boardroom and entered, closing the door behind me. While I was gone, Amy appeared to have opened every piece of packaging to explore what tools she had at her disposal. She looked up expectantly.

"Ready?" I asked.

"I guess so. I'm still not sure if this is going to be any help though. I've never drawn from... uh... inspiration like this before."

I sat at the head of the table. "I hear you, but just relax. If you can have fun with it, you'll do your best work. Draw anything that their pitches bring to mind, even if you want to draw something that looks like the crap emoticon. Anything."

"Really?"

"Absolutely. The people coming in are going to be all kinds of ages, from all walks of life, walking in here desperately hoping to impress us."

"Us? Or you?"

"Both of us. Think about it like this. Imagine somebody talking to a shrink, and the whole time, the shrink is taking down these mysterious notes. The content of those notes, the mystery of them, traumatize some people. That's you, sketching away on this pad they can't see. What about a lawyer, wondering if they've left their fly open and if so, has the courtroom sketch artist noticed? That's you. You're probably scarier to them than I am. At the same time, they've all got these young businesses or shiny new ideas that they're incredibly passionate about. If they're any good at pitching, that passion and enthusiasm will come through. Hopefully you can pick up on that and run with it."

"OK. This might be fun." She perked up.

"There you go. So, I say again… are you ready?"

"Yes."

"Make me believe it!"

"Yes!" she smiled.

"Alright."

I called the receptionist and had her send in the first group.

*****

It wasn't easy keeping a straight face, watching a balding man with flop-sweat stammering through his pitch while casting terrified glances in Amy's direction. The clack and scrape of her pencils against the paper wasn't exactly loud, but it was enough to tell that whatever she was doing, she was incredibly busy.

When I looked at her, she was staring at the man intently. Years ago, I watched a documentary that showed the difference between the way an artist looks at a subject and the way somebody who was crap at drawing looks at the same thing.

The way they did it was by having the artists and non-artists wear special glasses that tracked where their eyes looked when they had a model sitting in front of them and they were asked to draw the person's face. The eyes of the non-artists went all over the place. Artists concentrated on one tiny area at a time.

Amy had that same laser-focus. I couldn't remember if the documentary said it was innate or a trained skill, or both, but Amy certainly had it regardless.

"Thanks Marshall, you've given me a lot to think about. You've got a copy of the most recent financial documents for me?"

"Yes, sir," he said, circling the boardroom table to hand me the spiral-bound document.

"That's great. We'll be in touch."

I stood to shake his hand and then circled around behind Amy to see what the artist's impression looked like. She'd captured the sweat pouring off him really well.

The scene she'd drawn had him wearing a captain's hat on a shitty boat being dragged under by his own product at the end of the anchor chain. I laughed. Something told me that the financial documents would look pretty similar.

"That's just perfect. Only one more go to and then we'll break up for lunch."

"OK. This has been awesome! Are you sure this is an actual job that exists out there? Or are you just humoring me?"

I held up my hand in oath. "I promise. I've paid good money for this service, in other contexts."

A knock on the door turned my head in that direction in time to see it open and Kevin poke his head through. He looked about ready to explode into a shower of confetti.

"Anson's on the line. Hi, Amy."

"Hi." Amy gave a little wave.

"We can take it in my office," said Kevin. I gave him the thumbs up and he left.

"Holy shit. OK. OK. I got to take this, Amy… um… yeah, the last pitch is going to have to be rescheduled for another day. The boardroom is blocked out for the next hour, so you stay in here and do as many more sketches as you can, I'll come back after the call."

"No problem. Good luck!" Amy stood and pulled me down to give me a kiss on the cheek.

"Thanks, see you soon."

# Chapter 17

# Amy

Kris was gone for about half an hour before coming back and striding across the boardroom purposefully. I barely had time to get to my feet before he picked me up and whirled me around, almost laughing.

"Bad news?" I asked.

He gave me a big wet smacking kiss on the lips. "Terrible!" he said, then put me down on the ground again. "I know I said we'd only be in here this morning, but things have changed. I'm going to have to stay in the rest of the day. Let's get all your stuff into my office, you can work from there. You have enough ideas left to keep on going for the rest of the day?"

I'd woken today feeling somewhat down in the dumps, but been swept up in the excitement of just *drawing* all morning. Kris was clearly over the moon about something, and I wanted nothing more than to be happy for him, but I was feeling the pressure of the clock winding down on me now.

Kris set me up in his office, where he was in and out. Sometimes he went to Kevin's office, sometimes Kevin came to his.

I overheard things like "six hundred million dollars" and "obligation to provide consultancy services" but was mostly lost in my own little world. Each drawing I did sparked another memory about one of the presentations and gave me another idea for something to draw.

Kris was away from his office when somebody knocked on the door. I looked up and saw a man standing there with a piece of paper in his hand.

"Hey, where's Kris?" he asked, his eyes not rising above my breasts.

I picked up my art pad and crossed my arms over it in front of me like a shield, and his eyes finally met mine.

"I think he's with Kevin," I said.

"Oh right. Hey, you're Amy, aren't you?" he asked.

"Yeah... and you are?" I asked tentatively.

"I'm Daniel, I'm one of the partners here."

"Oh, hello. I thought there were only two partners?" I said. Kris had only spoken about himself and Kevin.

Daniel's face darkened scarily. "Well there's three."

"Sorry. I'm... I'm just a freelance designer Kris brought in. I guess he didn't explain the... uh... company structure to me very thoroughly."

Daniel rolled his eyes. "You're not a freelance designer. I know what you're selling."

Immediately, I felt about as insignificant as a bug. I wanted to shrink down to the size of one and scuttle away.

"I'm not sure what you mean," I said, barely able to speak above a squeaky whisper.

"Sure. I saw you on that website. Thought I might put a bid or two in myself, but didn't want to bankrupt old Kris there. So, uh... you done-"

"What the *fuck* are you doing?"

Daniel was yanked backwards out of the doorway by the collar and Kris shoved him to the side, out of sight. I heard harsh tones, but couldn't make out any words except for "motherfucker."

I felt numb. How many people knew why I was here? What about on Kris' yacht? Kim and Jane had seemed so nice, everybody had, but were they all talking behind my back about the slut in the black bikini?

I hadn't even considered the possibility if Kris telling anybody about our... arrangement. There was nothing stopping any customers of Innocence For Sale from doing so, I supposed, but I simply didn't think they would.

When Kris returned to his office, I couldn't bring my eyes any higher than my own hands resting on my art pad in front of me. He paused a few steps away.

"Amy... I'm sorry. He's such a fucking-"

"It's OK. You're the customer, you can tell whoever you want. The customer is always right... right?"

I was on the verge of crying. All the time we spent together, he never *felt* like a customer. That kiss at the bottom of the climbing wall wasn't from a customer. I hated to be reminded that this whole week was a fantasy. Hell, it wasn't even supposed to be *my* fantasy, no matter how much I was getting swept up in it.

"I'm sorry," he repeated.

"Who else knows? Just so I'm... prepared."

Kris hesitated. "Kevin knows. He's the one that told me about the service."

"Anybody else?"

"No."

"OK. I'll get back to work in a minute… I just need a-"

"Don't worry about that. I was just coming back here to suggest you head home for the night. It's been a long day and Kevin and I still have a lot to go over. Bernard can take you home, via anywhere you like for some food. I'll be back late."

"OK." I stood up robotically, suddenly desperate to get out of the office.

"You sure you're alright?" Kris asked.

"I'm fine," I lied.

*****

Back at Kris' penthouse, I almost cried myself to sleep on the couch. I'd been picturing myself heading home, dropping my suitcase and telling my mom to stop packing. We'd have a hug and celebrate, add another memory to the house that already held so many.

I thought I could be the heroine of my own story, but my time with Kris was more than half done now, and I hadn't managed to seal the deal yet. It now felt entirely possible that I could fail.

Something inside me twisted up and tried to wrench itself out of my body with a firm downward yank. I gritted my teeth against it, but my face contorted in an ugly grimace as the tears flowed.

This was supposed to be so easy. Arrive at the airport, get into his bed, close my eyes, open my legs and think of something else until he was finished.

Why did I have to have fun with him? Why did the time I spent with him have to feel so special? Why did he have me wrapped around his little finger, making me climax on command, but he wouldn't go all the way with me?

He *paid* to take my virginity, so why wasn't he doing it? What was going on?

I had no answers by the time Kris came through the door a little after midnight.

"Kris?" I called.

"Oh, hi. I didn't expect you to still be awake."

"Can you come sit with me?"

"Well... I dunno, I'm pretty tired, want to get some sleep as soon as I can, you know? Can we talk tomorrow? I'm really sorry about that shit at the office. I never spread the word around about why you were with me, how we met or anything, I promise you that. Daniel was just there when-"

"Please?" I patted the cushion next to me.

He loosened his tie and slumped a little, but came and sat on the couch. I grabbed one of his hands with both of mine and held it in my lap.

"This is kind of hard to say, I've been trying to think of words that don't sound dumb ever since I left the office. Um... Kris... I might be young, but I'm not stupid."

"I didn't think you were."

"I know something's going on here."

"What do you mean?"

"Why don't you want to... to have sex with me?"

"I told you, I just want to take my time. There's no hurry."

I frowned. "I don't think that's true. Are you having second thoughts about this whole thing? Have you decided you don't like the idea of... paying for it? I can understand that, I mean... I don't like the idea of *being* paid for it. But I wasn't lying yesterday. I like you. Nobody else has ever made me feel as sexy as you have. Can't we concentrate on that? The part of this that's real?"

"It's not that."

"Well, what? Do you have... a girlfriend somewhere? Fiancé? Are you feeling guilty about cheating on somebody?"

"No."

I paused for a long, uncomfortable while. "Was it something I did? You can tell me. I can be better."

Kris shot to his feet. "No! I don't have time for the Spanish Inquisition. Everything's fine. It's been a long day, I've got to get some sleep, I'll see you in the morning."

He stormed off to his room and my hands flopped back to my lap, unable to keep a hold of him. His door shut with a conclusiveness that couldn't have been any clearer if it could speak English.

After a few minutes, I stood and retreated to my room. I needed help, and there was only one person I could turn to.

I wrote an email to Ada on my phone, begging for some ideas, and sent it before getting ready for bed. For a couple hours, I tossed and turned, checking my phone what seemed like every few minutes. It was after 2am when I saw a reply.

*ada@adascott.com* *Subject: Re: Help!*

*Hi Amy,*

*This sure does sound strange, I've never come across any client behaving quite like this before. That said, you still have time to get through this, so don't panic yet.*

*Every man has a weakness when it comes to women, we just need to find out what his is. I promise you, there is something you can do that he will not be able to resist. You're an IFS girl, if you can't do it, then nobody can and the human race is probably doomed to go extinct due to lack of interest in breeding.*

*Below is my go-to list of kinks. You've got some outfits there with you, for some of the others you might need to improvise and find the right equipment. This should be more than enough to keep you busy today, but let me know how it goes and I'll get the brain trust working on the problem with some more suggestions for tomorrow...*

# Chapter 18

# Kris

"I could put a carrot in your ass."

Hands down, weirdest day of my life. I'd spent a good portion of the night tossing and turning, feeling guilty about everything that had happened with Amy and wondering how she was going to be when she emerged from her bedroom.

How badly had that cocksucker, Daniel, embarrassed her? How was my continued rejection affecting her?

I thought she might have been quiet and withdrawn. Maybe angry. Instead, she was like a kink-chameleon. Every quarter of an hour she was trying to entice me with one thing or another.

First thing in the morning I had a one-woman cheer squad pepping me up to eat my breakfast ("Give me a D!"). While I was going over some paperwork at my desk in my home office she was a sultry little secretary wanting to take DICKtation.

In any other week, I'd have taken her where she stood. This was no ordinary week though.

It only went downhill from there. I told her to put the fucking candle out before she dripped any hot wax on me. I had no interest in her dressing up in a full-body fox suit like the guy handing out pamphlets on the street corner. And now *this*. A carrot? In *my* ass?

"Would you like that?" she asked, looking at a vegetable stall across the street from the restaurant, while we waited for Bernard to bring the car.

"No! Hell no."

My car pulled up and Bernard rushed around to open the back door for us. Amy hopped in while I glanced around to make sure nobody had heard her last comments. The coast seemed clear.

"Where to next?" she asked.

"Dreamzone Fun Park," I said.

"I hear that place gets pretty busy. Crowded. So, in the middle of all those people, did you want to..."

I sighed. "No. First, I've hired the whole place out for just the two of us. Second... Amy... I'm still sorry about what happened yesterday. I'm sorry that anybody else knows about why you're with me this week. I've felt lucky to have you around and I wish we could have met another way. Can you please just... go back to being yourself?"

Amy slumped a little as she mulled it over. It might have been a dumb move on my part, asking her to ease back on this unattractive desperation and go back to the girl who had been driving me to breaking point for the past few days, but I missed her. It was that simple.

"Tell me I don't need to worry," said Amy.

"About what?"

"About anything I brought up last night. About anything I *didn't* bring up last night. Tell me you want me."

I resisted the urge to gulp, and took the easy out she unknowingly offered me. I wanted her. I didn't need to lie about that.

"I want you, Amy," I said.

"So, kiss me."

I leaned over and pulled her closer, my thumb stroking her cheek. Our lips touched and I felt her relaxing as the kiss deepened. She moved closer and cuddled up to me when our lips parted, and I draped my arm over her shoulder.

A fun park is a whole new experience when you have the entire place to yourself. There was nobody there except a skeleton staff to run the rides and serve us refreshments so we could simply concentrate on having some fun.

Best of all, Amy was back to being her regular sweet self. The sultry act was gone and her smile shone as bright as the fairground lights.

We crisscrossed over the entire fun park, going on rides in random order for a few hours before we retired to a merry-go-round with some ice cream cones. I held Amy's cone while she lifted her skirt a little to straddle the plastic horse, but she wouldn't relinquish the teddy bear I'd won for her.

Before she settled down and took her ice cream back, I caught a glimpse of the scars on her thigh again. Amy sat the bear in front of her and held on to the pole as the music started up. The fake horses moved up and down while the merry-go-round revolved.

"How did you get those scars on your leg?" I asked.

Amy's eyes shot down to check if they were showing, and then back up. "You don't wanna hear about that…"

"Why not?"

"Are they why you haven't… you know?"

"*Those*? No! Are you kidding? They're barely even noticeable. Go on, tell me."

"Well… I guess. It happened a long time ago, so I don't remember it totally clearly."

"That's OK."

Amy took a slow breath. "I was a little over three years old, so I've been sporting these beauties for a long time now. My mom had some friends with a daughter the same age as me, so one day we went to a playground. My mom was sitting in her wheelchair, of course, and the girl's mom was sitting on a bench, so the two of them could chat about whatever moms chat about."

"My mom said she used to talk about how much she missed sleep," I said.

"Maybe. I can't remember if I was even close enough to hear them talking, I was too busy anyway. I *do* remember what an *amazing* place this playground was. It was just a run of the mill playground like you'd see anywhere in the suburbs, you know, but for *me*, it was out of this world. My mom couldn't get around playgrounds easily in her chair, they've always got sand or bark or something and she couldn't keep up with me to catch me if I fell head-first off something."

"So you fell anyway?"

"No. We were having a great time, her dad was helping us out, playing with us and it was just… perfect, as far as I can remember. Then the three of us were standing on the ground at the bottom of the fireman's pole looking at something and I heard my mom scream 'Look out!' The next thing I knew, I heard this growl and the girl's dad lifted her off the ground. Out of nowhere, I felt this fire on my leg and I was yanked off my feet, something was shaking the life out of me. I don't really remember much of the rest of that day, but they said some stray dog attacked me."

"Fuck, Amy. That's terrible, but I'm glad it wasn't any worse. It could've been," I said.

"Yeah, true. I didn't feel like it at the time though. I played with that girl every now and then afterwards until the family moved away, but I remember not liking her very much."

"Why not?"

"Because... there wasn't a mark on her." Amy looked ashamed of herself. "I had these huge, at the time, *huge* tears in my skin and big ugly bruises that hurt *so* much, and she didn't have a mark on her. She had a daddy to love her, lift her up and keep her safe and I didn't. I was jealous."

After all the acting she'd done today, this was laying herself bare in just as personal way as the night she'd enforced the IFS inspection rules. She was emotionally naked, a lonely island in a sea of light and music from the merry-go-round. She was beautiful.

"Sorry. I haven't had a perfect life," Amy said.

I swung off my plastic horse and grabbed on to the pole of hers to steady myself. Carefully, so I didn't spill any ice cream on her teddy bear, I wrapped my other arm around her waist and gave her a squeeze as the horse moved up and down.

She smiled. "Thanks. I needed that."

# Chapter 19

## Amy

We finished our ride on the merry-go-round and shortly afterwards finished our ice creams too. Kris had his arm draped over my shoulders and I felt so safe, like he was protecting me from the dangers imagined from the past and any that might come up in the present too.

I stole a glance up at him as we walked and felt my heart flutter a little bit. He was a real mystery.

When we were just having fun, being ourselves, it was hard to believe he didn't feel that *click* between us. He ran for the hills when things heated up, but he never seemed more attracted to me than when I was just Amy, instead of Amy the expensive escort.

That was never more apparent than when I was trying to go through Ada's laundry list of things to try with him. Everything I did seemed to make it easier for him to put a wall up between us. Especially the suggestion of putting something in his ass. That one hit a particularly sour note, judging by the look on his face.

Of course, there was *one* thing from Ada's list that I hadn't tried yet. Even reading it had almost made my heart stop.

Yet, if Kris was really attracted to *me*, maybe it was exactly what I needed to do. I'd run from it for over two years. I'd suffered because of it, I'd hated myself because of it, I'd tried to cure myself of it, but before everything hit the fan, it had seemed like the most natural thing in the world to be turned on by.

No matter how I tried to convince myself otherwise, in those nights all alone in my bed, when I got all hot and bothered, my mind *always* strayed back to what got me in so much trouble. It always... did the job.

Those few seconds of calm before the storm would always be burned into my memory. I was fifteen years old, I had a great boyfriend, life was good.

His parents were out and we were fooling around in his room. I decided the time was right to lose my virginity, and I wanted to lose it playing out my favorite fantasy.

I got on my knees, called Brett "Daddy" in my cutest voice, and my world ended. In those seconds of silence, it began to dawn on me that I'd done something very, *very*, wrong.

His face contorted from excited, to confused, to disgusted and then he started yelling, backing away, calling me a fucking sick bitch, throwing my school bag at me and telling me to get the fuck out.

The bullying started on social media that night. School was unspeakably traumatic the next day. I had nowhere to hide, everybody knew what I'd done and everybody thought I was the most vile thing ever to crawl up out of a toilet.

Word spread from the students to the teachers, my mom was called in and I was interrogated in front of her, the principal, the guidance counsellor and several adults I didn't know, about whether I was being abused at home by somebody. I wanted to die.

Instead, I ran. No amount of lengthy speeches from the principal in the school assembly could stop all the whispers and the bullying; in fact, they only made it worse. So my mom let me change schools.

Our farm was more or less right in the middle of two towns, so I started afresh and did my best to bury my deepest desires under a ton of shame. It didn't work. They were always there no matter what.

Even with all that, Kris had almost managed to unwittingly uncover them on our second night together. What if he was the first person I'd ever met who I could *really* be myself with?

My heart thundered in my chest, trying to respond appropriately to the hope, excitement and panic the thought evoked. I looked up at Kris again and bit my bottom lip.

We passed a photo booth, one of the few things in the park that didn't require a bored-looking Dreamzone employee to operate. My skin was tingling and my knees felt weak when I tugged on his arm.

"Hey, let's try this."

"Really?"

"Yeah."

I entered the booth first and Kris came in after me, pulling the curtain closed behind him. Instead of a coin slot, this one accepted credit cards, and Kris held his up to the scanner after I touched the screen to begin.

A friendly voice started talking about the process for getting our photos, all the fun filters we could apply to them, and so on, but my mind was in another world entirely. Either I was about to humiliate myself again, or I was about to connect with a man on a level I hadn't dared hope for in years. It was either going to be the most shameful or the hottest moment of my life, and it was a coin toss.

The screen in front of us showed an image of us and indicated approximately where our faces should be to have them properly centered in the photos. His was too high and mine was too low, but I could see myself looking a little shell-shocked. It was now or never.

I slipped down to my knees in front of him, despite the cramped space, rested my hands on his thighs, and gave him my biggest puppy-dog eyes. Would he be the man to dominate me in exactly the way I always wanted?

"Amy! Not here, seriously, there's nothing but this flimsy curtain-"

"I've been a *very* good girl. For my treat, I want *you* to be my first, OK Daddy?"

His eyes widened. When they narrowed, would it be in lust or disgust?

My answer came first from a twitch in his pants, *then* the fire of lust in his eyes. Hope surged inside me. *That* was exactly what he wanted to hear from a girl on her knees in front of him.

"What... did you call me?" he asked.

"I called you, daddy." I smiled, "and you can do *anything* you want with me, OK?"

Kris let out a slow puff of air. "Anything, huh?"

"Of course!"

"You think you've been good enough for your treat?"

Cool relief washed over me, followed by searing hot lust. My cheeks burned red and I nodded silently.

If I wasn't so busy being turned on, I might have been happy enough to cry. My first attempt to explore my sexuality with a member of the opposite sex had ended up with it locked up in a cage where it rattled the bars every time my mind was quiet enough. Now I'd turned the key and stepped back from the door. Was it free? Or was this some kind of trick?

"Why don't you show me what a good girl you can be." Kris grabbed a fistful of hair at the back of my head and tugged his zip down with the other hand.

"OK, Daddy, anything for you," I said, happily.

Kris couldn't get his cock out quick enough, for either of us. After he freed it from his pants, it quickly throbbed to full mast and I couldn't help but marvel at it anew.

"I'm such a lucky little girl," I said.

"Fuckin' hell, that's hot, Amy."

Kris, still gripping his cock halfway, slapped my face with his hard length as the automated voice told us to smile for the camera. The way it hit my cheek sounded like a single person was applauding our performance.

My eyes half-closed and I tried to kiss and lick his cock each time it came into range. I got it a few times, and felt either my own saliva or his pre-cum cooling on my cheek with the next slap.

Tightening his grip on my hair, Kris aimed his cock at my mouth and his thick head forced its way between my lips, opening my mouth to make room for it. His masculine presence filled my mouth and my world, and I felt the tip brush up against the back of my throat.

I fought a pitched battle with my gag reflex, my eyes watering with the effort as he used his grip to move my lips up and down his length. Mercifully, he let me recover for a few seconds before the head of his cock hit the back of my throat again.

He pushed down on my head, holding the pressure for a second, before pulling out completely and letting me suck in as much air as I could. He slapped me with it again, this time it was positively soaked, and it splashed against my cheek, stinging a little thanks to its sheer weight.

"You like Daddy's big cock, Amy?" he growled.

"I *live* for Daddy's big cock," I gasped, a tear of happiness falling down my cheek.

The tear was probably just as much to do with my gag-reflex, but my joy was undeniable. I didn't have any time to debate myself on this philosophical position before he shoved his thick rod into my mouth again.

The automated voice told us to strike a pose, but Kris wasn't staying still for even a fraction of a second. His hand, which had been on his cock, curled around the back of my neck and he used his complete control of my head to hold me exactly where he wanted as he thrust his huge length in and out of my lips, pounding on the back of my throat.

His cock was a blur of motion beyond the tears welling up in my eyes, his thrusts past my lips moving so fast that they merged into a steady sensation. I held on to his thighs for dear life, feeling his muscles bulge while he fucked my face as hard as any daddy of my deepest fantasies ever had.

Timing my breathing between such frantic pounding against my throat was almost beyond me, but I managed to get enough air to stay conscious while Kris' cock swelled to what felt like diamond-hardness in my mouth.

He began groaning, a low primal growl that meant the same thing now as it did before language was invented. Pure lust. The mere sound of it made a spark of pleasure zap me between the legs and part of my brain noted that I could feel a distinct wetness down there.

He held his cock against my throat and I squeezed my eyes shut with the effort of this new battle in the war against my gag-reflex. His entire cock twitched and suddenly my mouth was flooded with his sperm.

Never in my wildest dreams did I imagine a man could cum so much, let alone on the first spurt, and it kept on coming. Not knowing what else to do, I tried to swallow and a second jet went straight down my throat. Most of the third spilled out of my mouth, down my chin, and fell down my top.

I could feel his semen, flowing down to my bra, slick against my skin, on my face and in my mouth. I was soaking in it, marked by it, *claimed* by him. My pussy was quivering with the need for attention.

Finally, he relaxed and I pulled back so his cock popped out of my mouth, temporarily increasing the flow of the rivulet of creamy cum flowing down my chin. I rested my head on it like it was the world's most perfect pillow, making a mess of the cheek he hadn't already cock-slapped me on, and looked up at him, panting.

I could feel his seed all over my face. "Thank you for making me so pretty, Daddy," I said.

# Chapter 20

# Kris

So that was what a million-dollar, plus generous tip, blowjob felt like. Watching my cock pistonning in and out of her mouth was like heaven on earth.

And yet... a seven-figure blowjob. Holy fuck. I'd lost control. Over a million to Kevin and another million plus if I couldn't get my money back from InnocenceForSale.com.

After she'd spent all day putting on those literal and metaphorical disguises, I could have been forgiven for thinking that was just another one... but it hadn't felt that way. Either she really loved pretending to be Daddy's little girl, it was my kryptonite, or both.

I'd never waited so long to fuck a girl before, and holy fuck had I unloaded on her. She was a mess of cum from her cheeks on down once my cock stopped twitching, a fucking beautiful sight.

No amount of napkins could completely handle the task. We tidied up as much as possible and left Dreamzone straight away so Amy could have a shower.

Blowing my load all over her restored some fraction of my tattered willpower, but if she had really pushed it, I probably wouldn't have been able to resist fucking her. As it was, I managed to bid her goodnight so I could retire to my room and ponder the reality that I was halfway to complete forfeiture of the bet.

Amy didn't seem to mind. Not in the way she had the previous nights, anyway. She had an air of euphoria about her and, unmistakably, confidence that was definitely a clear and present danger to the remaining half of my wager with Kevin.

Somehow, I slept like a baby. That blowjob certainly relieved some tension that had been building up.

When I woke, my brain went to work immediately, analyzing the situation. Tonight was Obvius.ly's celebration party for hitting twenty million monthly active subscribers, so the most perilous time of day was already going to be spent in public at a party.

With my newly-bolstered sense of willpower and keeping us busy during the day, I could get through this one last night. Tomorrow, another busy day, plus Amy would have to pack for her late-night flight.

I could do this.

When Amy emerged from her room, she was on top of the world, humming with excitement. I didn't even have a chance to lay out a plan for the day before she asked if it would be OK for her to go shopping alone.

Deep down, I knew she must have had her reasons, but it felt like a get out of jail free card at the time. The party would run late, so I'd still be spending plenty of time with her.

The only card of mine she accepted was the key card so she could get back in and she left after giving me a happy little peck on the cheek. I shrugged at the back of the closed door and went to my home office.

The instant I showed up online, I had a video call from Kevin. I put on my headset and accepted the call.

"Morning, you rich motherfucker!" said Kevin.

"Morning."

"Come on now, where's the enthusiasm?"

"Fuck you," I said, pulling a checkbook out of my drawer.

"Oh, you haven't seen it?"

I glanced up at the screen. "Seen what?"

"Five minutes ago. Check your mail."

I brought up my email on a second screen and saw that Anson Allen had sent a message, with the subject "Re: Contract Amendments." I looked back at Kevin's smiling face, then opened the email.

With each line I read, the sense of triumph built. My heart was thundering in my ears and I didn't even realize I'd stood to my feet until I heard Kevin laughing.

"There it is! That's more like it!" he said.

I sat down again, holding my finger up at the email. "He's coming tonight, to the party, to sign in person?"

"Yes! It's really happening. So, how does it feel?"

"Um... how the fuck do you think it feels? Feels great!" I said.

"I mean, specifically, to be a billionaire?"

"Oh." I dragged the word out and sat back in my chair, tenting my fingers in front of me and looking off into the distance dramatically.

"Don't keep me in suspense."

I leaned forward again and wrote him his check for one million one hundred and eighty thousand dollars. "Well, son, it feels like I'm getting what I deserve after many years of hard work. I want you to know that, even though I'm a much better person now, I won't let it go to my head or change me in any way. We'll still go golfing on Sundays even though now I'll be using you as my tee."

"Look at me now, ma."

"If you put in the work, you too can achieve greatness. So, with that in mind, I'd like to offer you a little contribution to help you on your way to financial independence." I held the check up to the camera so he could see it.

"Aha! I fucking knew it! You couldn't keep your dick out of her. That's two in a row. Man, this day just couldn't get any better."

"I didn't fuck her."

"Then..." he held his hands up in confusion.

"She... uh... finished what she started the other day."

"Oh. Right. Well, you might as well fuck her now. I don't want any technicalities ruining the record of this wondrous occasion."

"Thanks for the advice, but my head's clear now. I can make it until tomorrow night."

"I dunno, something tells me you might feel like celebrating," Kevin said.

"Who me? No chance, Kevin 'Hollow Victory' Grant. I'll see you tonight."

"Alright, hey, think Anson would be up to signing the contract on stage?"

"Maybe, very theatrical," I said.

"I'll run it past him. Catch you later."

"Bye."

I tucked Kevin's check into my wallet as I read Anson's email again. He was right, this was cause for celebration if anything ever was. I just wished I could have celebrated my largest ever exit properly with Amy.

For the next couple of hours, I reworked my speech so I could speak a little about the acquisition. Kevin confirmed Anson would be happy to seal the deal in front of all the attending employees, so I made an allowance for that too.

It was still well before lunch when Amy returned. I caught a glimpse of her through my door, and I caught her eye too.

"Hi! I'll be there in a minute," she called.

I could see she was carrying a couple shopping bags, but I couldn't make out what store they were from at this distance. I saved my speech and read over the changes while I waited for Amy, prepared to steer us straight back out the door as soon as humanly possible.

She was gone for several minutes. When I heard the door to her room open, I saved my speech again and stood, reaching for my jacket. My fingers lost the dexterity required to pick it up when I saw her leaning against the doorframe of my office though.

The first thing I saw was that she was hugging the teddy bear I won her last night with one arm while she twirled a pigtail around the finger of her opposite hand. Her legs were covered up to mid-thigh with some knee socks, leaving a tantalizing band of smooth skin between the tops of those and the hem of her short pleated skirt.

Her tank top hugged her body almost skintight and left no doubt as to whether she was wearing a bra underneath. Amy's nipples poked at the material, and all I wanted to do was feel her breasts in the palms of my hands, to squeeze those nipples until she breathlessly panted my name.

"I've got a present for you, Daddy," she said in the most innocent voice I'd ever heard.

I was about to lose another million dollars.

# Chapter 21

# Amy

It took me longer than I wanted to find everything I needed. I didn't need much, but being unfamiliar with the area I didn't know exactly where to go.

Some ribbons to tie my hair in pretty pigtails, some knee socks and a pleated skirt. I already had the tank top and Kris won the teddy bear for me. It was perfect. It was my dream come true, and the way Kris closed the distance between us, I thought it must have been his dream come true as well.

Kris reached out and curled his fingers around the back of my neck, pulling me into a kiss. I went up on my toes and his other hand squeezed my ass *tight* while he stole my breath.

He pushed me to the side and then held me against the wall with his entire body, one knee sneaking between mine so I had to part my legs a little. I could feel the material of his pant leg on the bare skin of my inner thighs above my knee socks, pushing my already short skirt up.

"What have you got for me, Amy?" he asked.

"You're so good to me, Daddy, I want you to be happy."

"What do you think would make me happy?"

"I thought, maybe, you could use me. I'm *really* tight, Daddy. Would that make you happy?"

His huge hard cock pressed against my inner thighs, trapped down his pants leg as it hardened. I whimpered quietly, and he knew why.

"You think you can take it, little girl?" he asked.

"I don't know," I said, truthfully, "but I want you inside me, even if it hurts."

"If I start, I don't know if I can stop."

"I won't want you to stop, Daddy."

Kris kissed me again, a deeper and more powerful kiss than I ever dreamed possible, and lifted me off my feet so suddenly that I almost dropped my teddy bear. I wrapped my legs around his waist and he held me off the ground by my ass, carrying me out of his office.

He must have had the layout of his penthouse committed in perfect detail to his memory, otherwise I had no idea how he navigated his way through while carrying me and indulging me with *that* kind of kiss. Kris bent over and I felt the couch under my back as he climbed on top of me.

Curling one arm behind my neck, he held me close while reaching between our bodies and into his pants. With a little wiggle and yank, he adjusted himself so his big cock was freed from his pants leg. When he pushed himself against me, I could feel that big bulge pushing my panties into my slit.

"I love your cock *so much*, Daddy," I breathed, bucking my hips so I could feel it sliding along my folds with only a few layers of material between us.

"Holy fuck, Amy, I'm going to *ruin* you."

"Yes please!"

Kris disentangled himself from my legs and stood to remove his clothes. I watched, entranced, as he pulled off his shirt and I could once again feast my eyes on that hard physique.

His every movement was depraved poetry in motion. My captivated attention was no doubt written plainly on my face as I twirled a pigtail around and held my breath while he undid his pants.

When he hooked his thumbs inside the waistband and pulled his pants and underwear down in a single motion, his glorious cock sprang free and tilted like the world's thickest dowsing rod in my direction. It was a work of art, and my legs parted a little at the sight of it.

They parted even further when he came closer, but instead of moving between them, he straddled my chest. From this perspective, his cock towered huge and menacing over me. It was incredible to think that the last time I'd seen it, it had just finished cumming in my mouth and all over my face.

Me. *I* had given Kris all that pleasure. *I* had turned him on enough to get over whatever hang-ups he had about this arrangement. I could do it again, but this time all that cum would be inside me and by the end of it I wouldn't be a virgin anymore.

Kris pulled my tank top up over my tits and squeezed them with both hands, pushing them up and together to create deep cleavage out of even my modest size. When he let them spring back to their natural shape, he pinched my nipples between his finger and thumb.

Rolling them both until I was almost at the point of pain, he then released and flicked his thumb across one. I moaned and reached around his thighs, pulling my panties aside with one hand so I could touch myself with the other.

Kris pulled my teddy bear out from the crook of my arm and shoved it under my head like a teddy-pillow before grasping his shaft and aiming it at my mouth. I licked my lips and opened my mouth, trying to think of how I could stop him if he really got going like at Dreamzone. The last thing I wanted was for him to waste his sperm in my mouth.

His balls trailed lightly up my chest between my breasts as the tip of his cock passed my lips. I moaned long and hard, right on the head of his cock, and Kris sucked air in between his teeth.

Just buying what I needed for my outfit had made me excited beyond belief. Even the faint stimulation of walking around with my panties brushing against my sex had been a thrill under the circumstances, and I could feel the evidence of that arousal now as I spread my own slickness over my clit.

Kris thrust his cock in and out of my mouth, watching my face intently as he did so. My virginal self-doubts tried to make me feel embarrassed, but he looked so turned on and his cock was so hard that it was an emotion that couldn't stick.

"Fuck you look beautiful sucking my cock, Princess," said Kris.

I hummed "Thank you, Daddy," on his cock and he groaned in satisfaction.

With his cock gathering speed in my mouth, I writhed under him. My finger flicked back and forth across my clit, dipping into my virgin entrance every now and then to spread out more of my sweet nectar.

Every time I strained against him, a humming energy seemed to grow in my muscles, especially in my navel area. My breath started catching every time I exhaled, moaning harder and harder as my pleasure grew.

Kris' cock was thrusting harder and deeper, brushing against the back of my throat each time now, but I was too preoccupied with my own approaching climax to be concerned by it or how to stop him cumming in my mouth. Just when I thought I was going to push myself over the edge, Kris grabbed my wrists and pulled my hands away from my pussy.

My eyes fluttered and focused on his face. He had his cock pressed hard against the back of my throat, so I couldn't pout the way I wanted to but I at least tried to look as put out as I could.

"Don't you dare, Amy. The next time you cum, I want to feel that pussy of yours gripping my cock for all its worth."

All disappointment evaporated in an instant and I nodded before he withdrew his thick shaft from my mouth. A rivulet of saliva and pre-cum dribbled down my chin, but I couldn't wipe it away because Kris still had a hold of my wrists. He sucked my juices off my fingers one by one and then moved back to get between my legs.

# Chapter 22

# Amy

Kris' cock stood straight and hard, the tip glistening with saliva and pre-cum, reminding me to wipe my chin. I could feel the cool air on the wetness between my legs and gulped nervously.

"Do you think it'll fit, Daddy?" I asked.

"I'll make it fit."

Reaching up my skirt and sliding his hands over my ass, he hooked his fingers into the waistband of my panties and pulled them off. I lifted my legs and pointed my toes so he could cast them away.

He curled his arm around my right leg and bent down to tease the back of my knee with licks and kisses, his well-manicured stubble just the right length to add some tingle to proceedings. I braced my hands against the cushions, and uttered a sound of utterly pleasured gibberish for a second before attempting to clamp my mouth shut.

Kris tortured me with his attention, which felt like a cross between a tickle, a gentle stroke of my clit and a passionate kiss all rolled into one. I was barely in control of my own muscles when he finally relented and let my leg rest on his shoulder, twitching slightly.

"I think it's time to take what's mine, little girl," Kris said with a quiet growl around the edge of his voice.

"No matter what I scream, don't stop, Daddy. OK?"

"I'm gonna fuck you the way a sexy little bitch like you deserves."

Grasping his hard cock, his muscles flexing and so clearly defined, he aimed his hard length down at my slit and I gasped when I felt the tip of it touch my virgin folds. I braced my hands on the couch again, trying to stop myself from hyperventilating.

This was *it*, a man had his cock between my legs, I could *feel* him against my entrance. He was impossibly big, impossibly *hard* and masculine. It was terrifying and addictive. I needed more.

"Uhn!" I cried out as Kris put some pressure on.

He'd made me so wet that my labia was immediately pushed aside, sliding over the head of his cock as my lips had so recently. However, unlike my mouth, my pussy soon reached its limits, stretched out to a tight ring of fire around his girth.

"Ow! Owowow! Ow, Daddy... it's so big!"

"Good girl, you're so fucking hot, Amy."

I bit my lower lip as he pushed forward even harder. He placed his hand on my mound and gently rubbed my clit with his thumb.

My mind was blown. It was too much sensation coming from one area of my body. Pleasure and pain blurred and merged together into some new kind of fire between my legs.

The harder he pushed, the faster he rubbed my clit, masking the pain of his size forcing its way into my tight opening. To my surprise, despite the anxiety, I felt the orgasm Kris had stopped me from giving myself building again already.

Suddenly, I felt the head of his cock slip inside me to press against my hymen and I yelped in response, with no hope to halt the hyperventilation now. I needed more air than I could possibly breathe in.

Kris' thumb moved so fast it was practically humming on my clit and, with a jerk of his hips, he pushed forward to tear through the thin evidence of my virginity. It was one more intense sensation added to the melting pot and it started a chain reaction of ecstasy fluttering through my body.

He'd told me that the next orgasm I had would be with my pussy gripping his cock, but he was only barely correct. My virginal tunnel gripped and released him with each wave of bliss as he slowly forced more and more of his thickness into my untouched depths.

Every part of me that he claimed by virtue of discovery, by being the first man to touch me there, set off another cascade of pleasure that flowed from my pussy to my clit and echoed out to the tips of my fingers and toes. Kris only paused his strumming of my clit a couple of times to push my most sensitive spot against the advancing shaft of his cock, using it to pleasure me further.

I shut my eyes and it felt like my spirit was soaring in the clouds somewhere, vaguely tethered to my body by some cord of energy. It was beautiful up there, and I even got butterflies in my stomach when I started to float back down.

When I opened my eyes, I was back in Kris' penthouse and he had his full length buried in my newly deflowered pussy. I felt his balls resting on my ass and the tip of his cock faintly brushing my cervix. It was like we were custom-made for each other, he fit that snugly inside me.

My spirit threatened to take flight again as he started moving inside me, sawing his thick cock in and out. He leaned forward and I wrapped my arms around his neck, holding on for dear life and smiling from ear to ear with my eyes half closed.

I'd done it. No matter what happened from here on, I'd saved the farm. My virginity belonged to Kris forever, and I'd never met anybody I wanted to have it more. A good man, hot as hell, who reciprocated and fulfilled my dirty fantasy. A girl could do a lot worse for her first.

*I love you!*

My heart stopped at the sudden outburst from the crazy voice in my head. He was everything I'd just thought… but I wasn't allowed to love him. I must have been confusing *grateful* with love. Still, it was a sweet temptation to let my mind wander down that path. To think I was losing my virginity to the man I loved.

Kris quickly increased the power and pace of his thrusts, pounding me into the couch. Every time his balls slapped on my ass I was unimaginably *filled* with cock, stretched to my limit, burning with torturous pleasure.

I couldn't help but whimper and moan in time with his jack-hammering cock, the impact forced these little noises out of me and I was helpless to stop it. His rock-hard muscles flexed and relaxed with the unrelenting power of hydraulic machinery, powering his thick length into my depths over and over again.

Hanging on with one arm around his neck, I peeked out at the side of his head from the corner of my eye as if I might be doing something naughty, then let my other hand roam down his back towards his ass. Feeling that powerful muscle squeeze and release was hypnotic, I could have groped him forever, if I was given that much time.

Kris seemed to take my roaming hand as an invitation to fuck me even harder, and I quickly brought my arm back to his neck just to hold on for dear life. My pussy was a blur of sensation as he pistonned his entire length into me.

My toes curled gleefully when he kissed my neck, his hard cock thrusting with uninterrupted rhythm. His power rocked my entire body, even *my* perky little breasts were shaking with the force of his fucking.

"So *good*, Daddy."

I couldn't make any more sense than that. Even with such a short sentence, the impact of his body against mine made my voice shake comically.

The fire between my legs was starting to thrum with the kind of energy I was starting to get used to whenever Kris touched me there. I couldn't believe my luck. Twice in one session, was that *normal?*

Kris pushed our upper bodies off the couch and then pulled my arms away from his neck. I flopped back down, panting, and felt the way the different posture made his cock rub the front wall of my vagina.

He shuffled backwards, dragging me with him, until he stepped off the edge of the couch and pulled me so my ass was on the armrest. Manhandling my legs, he spun me around without taking his cock out of my pussy so I was bent over the armrest, presenting my pussy to him to fuck as hard as he wanted.

*Smack!*

My ass cheek stung as he brought his hand down firmly upon it and my head whipped around fast enough that I could feel my pigtails flying. He squeezed the spot he'd just hit, my skin sensitive to the touch, and resumed the frenzied pace he'd interrupted so he could change positions.

The armrest kept me right where Kris wanted me, without the bounce the cushions had provided. If he was fucking me the way a sexy little bitch deserved... I must have been a *very* sexy little bitch.

*Smack!*

I gasped as he spanked the exact same spot again, and reached forward to grab my teddy bear, pulling it back to me. Turning my head to look at Kris over my shoulder once more, I used the teddy bear partly as a pillow and partly just as something to hug.

Kris was a vision of masculine perfection. I could hardly believe that *he* was inside me, making me feel *so good*.

The impending climax that had started to fade during the change of positions began to rise again. I moaned louder with each thrust, squeezing my teddy bear with my arm and Kris' cock with my pussy as I started to lose control.

"I'm cumming for you, Daddy!"

The last syllable stretched out a little as a wave of ecstasy robbed me of my ability to speak and my eyes rolled back in my head. Pure thrumming bliss concentrated on my clit and pulsed out to my stomach, where it spread out to the tips of my fingers and toes, while my pussy tingled with his every thrust.

I felt Kris' cock swell and then a hot spurt of cum right on my cervix, and I felt my jaw drop at the mid-orgasm realization of what was happening. His creamy load of semen was being pumped inside of me, where it might have made a baby if I hadn't gone on the pill in advance of this week.

Kris' pace slowed, but he put every ounce of strength he could into each thrust, bringing our bodies together with a loud slap each time. By the time he was almost stopped completely, I could feel his seed leaking down the inside of my legs, there was just too much for one teen girl to contain.

He collapsed on top of me and nuzzled his way between my teddy bear and me so he could kiss me on the lips. I craned my neck to kiss him back with all the enthusiasm I could muster in my exhaustion.

"Thank you, Daddy," I whispered.

# Chapter 23

# Kris

The couch would never be the same again, and I was completely and utterly drained. I couldn't remember ever feeling so peaceful and satisfied in my entire life.

After fucking her brains out on the couch, we moved to the shower to clean up and ended up fucking again. Then *again* on her bed when we came out, before a second shower, and now we were cuddled up under a sheet on my bed, the first time she'd been in my room since arriving.

The room was quiet like when you step outside after a concert. I didn't have the ringing in my ears, it was simply that everything seemed so still compared with what had happened immediately beforehand.

Every word we spoke hung in the air with crystal clarity in that stillness. Her every movement against my body sent a warm shiver of memory down my spine, especially the way she trailed her fingers over my chest and abs, mesmerized by the bumps and grooves of my muscles and patterns of my tattoos.

This alone was worth the two million plus dollars I'd lost on my wager, never mind the unparalleled sex that had preceded it. I wanted to hold Amy forever.

Amy lifted herself up to kiss my cheek before flopping back down into her spot with her head resting on my shoulder and my arm around her.

"That was... incredible," she said, quietly.

"That was, hands down, the best sex of my life," I said.

"I was... OK?"

"Better than all the others combined. How in the hell did you manage to keep the guys away from you back home?"

"I was, usually, in a relationship."

"Well... how did you keep your *boyfriends* away from you? If you'd called him Daddy I bet you'd have had him eating out of the palm of your hand."

Amy grimaced. "It... didn't work like that with my boyfriend. When I was fifteen, I'd been with him for a while, but things were getting... you know, intimate. I said it and he thought it was the most disgusting idea he ever heard. He humiliated me at school. I had to *change* schools, delete all social media. It was... awful. I spent the last few years ashamed of who I was, what I liked. I'm so glad I found you."

"What kind of a weirdo wouldn't want you to do that? It's nothing to be embarrassed about."

"Well, I was. What was *your* most embarrassing moment?"

"Um..."

"Go on," she said.

"Uh... well... OK. I got one."

Amy snuggled in with a little smile on her face.

"This happened a long time ago now. My grandmother, my dad's mom, was getting older and she was in and out of hospital. My aunt was living with her, just so she always had somebody around to help out, but we were all kind of bracing ourselves for bad news. She was in her eighties so, you know, anything can happen at that age."

The smile had dropped from Amy's face and her brow was knitted a little in concern.

"So, anyway, at the time my old phone had just died. It stopped charging for some reason. It was just a cheap pay-as-you-go kind of thing, so I took the sim card out and stuck it in a new one for fifteen bucks."

"You didn't just buy the phone company?" she asked.

"No, this was back in the day."

"Oh, back in the day. Alright."

"Mmmhmm. The problem with this was that, although I kept the same number, I lost all my phone contacts. I didn't worry too much about it, figured it'd be like a spring clean of contacts I didn't need anymore and the people I did want I'd just pick them back up again as I went."

Amy grabbed my hand and pulled my arm tighter around her, putting my palm on her breast before going back to tracing my tattoos with her finger as she listened.

"One night, I got a text message. It said "Just letting you know, Mom died last night" and it was from a number I didn't have saved in my phone as yet."

"Your... aunt then? I'm sorry, by the way. Seems like something that maybe deserved a phone call. Were you close to your grandmother?"

"Well, hold your horses there. I thought it was more phone call kind of news as well, but then I thought, however close I was to my grandmother, my aunt was closer. You know, cause of living together and straight up just because they were mother and daughter. I thought, who knows how much she's got on her plate to deal with now, maybe this is a mass text to notify a bunch of people."

"That's true, I suppose."

"So, I texted back saying I was sorry to hear it and asking if she needed any help with anything. I got a reply a while later saying thanks but everything is basically under control."

"OK."

"Then, I decided to wait for a while. I thought, odds were, my aunt was probably having a lot of phone calls with her siblings, which obviously included my dad."

"How many siblings?"

"She has a sister and two brothers."

Amy nodded.

"So, I think it was about an hour or two later, I hadn't heard anything else, so I decided it was time to give my dad a call. He answered, and I'm all doing my best to have the most sympathetic tone possible, so I said something like hi, how are you doing?" I said, holding my hand out as if I needed it to keep my balance while walking on eggshells. "He said "Great!" and he was just so… upbeat, I was kind of taken by surprise. I thought to myself "Wow… this guy's a real trooper.""

Amy's brow knitted in confusion again.

"I think the next thing I told him was that he sounded like he was coping pretty well, you know, considering… and he said, 'Considering what?' and my heart just dropped. It dawned on me that he hadn't heard yet, you know?"

"Oh, no…"

"Yeah… so… oh fuckin' hell, I can still remember this bit just fine. I said I got a text from Patti earlier and she said Nana died."

"That's what I called my nana too," said Amy. "How did he take it?"

"He was like '*What!?*' and I said 'Yeah... Patti didn't call you?' Well, apparently not, so he said he was going to call her and find out what was going on."

"Mmmph. Yeah, that's pretty rough, but not sure if I'd call it embarrassing."

"Uh... it doesn't end there."

"Oh... how does it end?"

"See... my dad called me back after a few minutes. He'd been in touch with Patti... and my nana. She was just fine."

"Uh..."

"It turned out that the text I'd received was sent to the wrong number! I found out by giving them a call and finding out that, in fact, this was not my aunt's phone number. So... my most embarrassing moment was telling my dad that his mom was dead and being wrong about it."

Amy's face went from disbelief to shocked and quickly settled on a big silly grin before she let out a kind of gigglesnort. "I'm sorry... that's not funny."

The way her last word was distorted by laughter made me doubt the truth of the statement. "It's OK. It was a long time ago now. I was... *mortified* back then, but time heals all wounds so they say."

"Wow."

"My dad never told my aunt or nana why he called that night. It's been our little secret for, what, about fifteen years. You're the first one I ever told about it."

"Aw." Amy gave me a little squeeze.

I leaned down and kissed her on the forehead, then spent some time stroking her hair with my thumb. It felt so fucking weird to have fucked her and still want her around more than ever, but I couldn't get enough.

Was she the first woman I'd slept with that I hadn't fucked at the first possible opportunity? I couldn't remember another, if I had. Maybe what I was feeling was the simple result of spending any time with her before fucking, but *damn* it felt good.

"How did you end up here?" I asked, thinking out loud.

Amy sighed. "I don't know, my head's still spinning."

"I mean, you're a beautiful young woman, promising artist, smart and full of life, your family owns a farm... what led you to be on that website?"

Amy sighed again. "The bank."

"Hmm?"

"The bank owns all too much of the farm."

"Oh, mortgage payments?"

"Yeah... um... you sure you want to hear this? Ada said it's not... sexy to talk about my problems."

"You couldn't be unattractive if you tried. I want to know *you*. So, go on, spit it out."

"If you *insist*. Where do I start... uh... well, the farm has been in my family, on my dad's side, for generations, but when my parents had that accident... it kind of started knocking over a few really crappy dominos. All I know is what my mom told me, so I don't know if I have this all in the right order, but because they were in that accident and my dad wasn't around to manage the farm, we lost most of the crop that year, I don't know why. The next year, a neighbor pitched in and did what he could to help us out, but there was a flood and we lost most of that crop too. With my mom's medical bills piling up, she had no choice but to borrow against the farm. It got us through, but by this time it was a few years since the accident, nobody was really willing to work the farm for free because they had their own lives to run. So, what my mom did then was lease out the farm to somebody who was willing to work it, while keeping us in the house."

"That makes sense," I said.

"Yeah, but the lease income isn't as much as it would have been if my dad was around, or if mom was able to run the farm."

"No, that makes sense too."

"It just wasn't enough to keep up with everything that needed to be paid. The global financial crisis didn't help anything, of course, when that stomped through our lives. We've been through refinancing, and payment plans, but back in February they just... stopped listening. We had to pay up or get out."

"They can be real assholes."

"Yeah. I went crying to my boyfriend and found him sleeping with another girl."

"Not the one who..."

"No, this is the one after that. It was a... pretty bad day. I blamed myself at the time, thought I must have needed more patience than any man had. Later I found out that he never thought being my boyfriend was any reason for him to stop sleeping with other girls. So, unbeknownst to me, I was kind of a joke in certain circles for my entire time at that school."

"Motherfuckers."

"Hmm. Yeah. So. Do you have a... home?" she asked.

I gave a vague gesture to indicate my penthouse and raised an eyebrow.

"No. You *live* here, but you haven't been here long, you said you've got a lease on it so you know when you're probably going to leave. What about, like, a place where you grew up? A *home* home."

"Nah, my parents were lifelong renters until I bought them a house a while back. We moved around a lot while I was growing up. It sucked."

"Oh. Well, maybe you won't *get* this, but the farm... that farmhouse, is *magic*. There's all these marks on the doorframes." Amy held up her hand and did little sideways chopping motions, each higher than the one before. "They go up until somewhere between four and five feet and then, mostly, they stop. These are the marks left by my family, showing how high this or that kid was when they were various ages. I can see how tall my great aunt was when she was three and a half years old by going to the right door in my house."

"Wow."

"I can *feel* how proud her parents were, how proud *she* was about being such a big girl, I can imagine how she must have compared herself against her brother, who's marked on the same doorframe."

Amy's eyes were getting glassy as she explained, and I held her all the tighter.

"There's one doorframe that shows how tall *I* was when I was growing up. The first mark says 'Amy – 1 Year' and the handwriting is different than all the other marks, because it's the only one written by my dad. I only learned how to stand and walk a little while before he died. There's nowhere, *nowhere*, in the entire world like that house."

"It sounds... beautiful," I said.

Amy let a few tears fall freely, then wiped one eye with the back of her hand, and the other on my chest.

"My family *built* that house, they lived and loved in that house forever, and that night, the day the letter arrived from the bank and I was all alone because my boyfriend is a motherfucking asshole, I was like 'No, no, no, no!'" Amy's fist beat on an invisible wall. "'Not on my watch. We will *not* lose it on *my* watch.'"

"So you stumbled across the Innocence For Sale site?"

"Not yet. I tried to shop around with other banks to buy us some time, but they wouldn't touch us with a fifty foot pole, I set up a crowdsourcing page to ask for donations, but the only people who cared enough were my aunt and uncle who donated, like, fifty bucks to hopefully get the thing rolling and they're *still* the only contributors, they have their own financial problems. It took a couple weeks before I found IFS. That's what we *in the biz* call it, IFS." Amy joked and wiped her eyes.

"Wow. What was it like, you know, signing up for all that?"

"So, *so*, weird. Ada's got all these forms. For personality tests, personal history, general information, whatever. I remember this part of one form, it was like... a checklist of all the things I'd be willing to do with a... um... winning bidder. Some of them were pre-checked, like, compulsory things like 'Vaginal Intercourse', and it was such a technical term, but then there was another one pre-checked and it was 'Creampie' and I had to ask her what on earth that was."

I laughed so much that Amy had to push herself up on her elbow because her head was getting shaken around too much while resting on my shoulder.

"I guess *you* know what that is then," she said.

"Yup."

"*How?*"

"I'm a guy who has the internet," I said.

"OK, so your internet is different to mine. Why on earth do they call it a creampie when a man cums inside a woman? No! Don't answer. I don't want to know!"

I laughed some more, but managed to settle down when she rested her head on my shoulder again and pulled my arm around tightly.

"I bet you would have had problems creating a business if you had to use *that* word from that random word generator," she said. "Annoying Creampie Jamming."

I absolutely lost my mind laughing, but this time Amy joined in.

"I don't know," I said. "Half of the commerce on the internet seems to have something to do with creampies, so it's a popular... uh... product."

"I weep for humanity."

"So, problem solved now. Does your mom know what you're doing?"

"Hell no!"

"How are you going to explain how you came up with all that money?"

"I'm going to tell her that some Good Samaritan gave us everything we needed on the crowdfunding site. She doesn't really get the internet, so I probably won't have to face an expert, shall we say, cross-examination."

I slipped my free arm under the sheet and curled it around the small of her back, pulling her into a hug, and kissed her on the forehead. Say what you wanted about the escort industry as a whole, this was a sexy, brilliant, determined girl who did what she had to do to save what was important to her.

Admirable was too weak a word to describe her. She was exquisite. Too good for just one week. Too good for any finite amount of time. It terrified me to sense the fight inside myself, trying to avoid putting a label on the emotions I felt when I looked at her, or touched her, or *thought* about her. *Fuck*. I loved this girl.

The seed planted by her pure beauty had been nurtured by everything she said and did. Despite our situation not being what you could call fertile ground, despite *me* not being fertile ground, for love, there it was. I fucking loved this girl.

"Amy?"

"Hmm?"

"I was thinking... after tomorrow... I don't want you to go."

I'd never put any thought or effort into finding a girl who was good for more than one night of fun before they were cast out of my life. The words hanging on my lips now had always been considered the ones suckers said to women when they couldn't get any other pussy. It was different with Amy. She made other girls irrelevant.

"I love you," I said.

Amy raised her head and looked at me like I'd told her the pilots had bailed and it was up to her to land the plane.

"Stay with me," I said.

# Chapter 24

## Amy

I opened and closed my mouth like a fish out of water when Kris told me he loved me and wanted me to stay with him. What he was asking ran contrary to every scrap of common sense I had and every warning Ada had given. If I could find a way to let him down gently, I should.

That was a good reason to stay silent and choose my words carefully, but it wasn't the *real* one. He said he *loved* me. I didn't know how much I'd wanted to hear that until the words hit my ears.

I'd heard it from my mom, my aunt too, but I'd never heard it from my previous boyfriends, or any man. It was different somehow, the *way* he said it.

His voice was so *deep*, I could feel his chest rumbling when he spoke. His words had a physical presence, and I didn't want to speak, to banish those special words to a memory. I wanted to bask in them for as long as I could. I waited over eighteen years to hear words like that for the first time. Who knew how long I might have to wait to hear them again?

The words were scary, even more so because they'd echoed in my own head earlier. What chance would an odd couple like us have?

It wasn't easy to judge time under the circumstances, but a reasonable person could probably describe it as an awkward amount of silence by the time Kris spoke again.

"It's alright, you don't have to decide now. Just think about it. We've got to start getting ready for the party anyway."

"OK. The party. Right."

Whatever time was doing now, it had certainly flown while Kris had taken my virginity all over the penthouse. Heading back to my room to figure out what I was going to wear, I was painfully aware of the need to walk a little bow-legged. I hoped that would ease off before the party.

With a little soothing moisturizer and my silkiest pair of panties, my problem was solved by the time we arrived. I felt like a celebrity when the car pulled up and we stepped out on to a red carpet. Some people, Obvius.ly employees who had walked from nearby I supposed, even cheered jokingly.

The party was being held in the function room of the Grand Altier Hotel not too far from Kris' building. It had a stage, a dancefloor, a buffet-style selection of food along one wall, and several tables with assigned seating.

We sat at the main table, of course, due to Kris' position in the company. To my embarrassment, though, that meant the other founders, Kevin and Daniel, were also placed there. The other two people in this world who knew exactly why I was even here this week. Assuming they hadn't told anybody else.

Kevin had a date, but Daniel didn't, and every time I looked in his direction I saw him quickly glance away. There was something about his expression that made me really uncomfortable. I tried to stay as close to Kris as I could, but on a night like this, he was being pulled in a thousand different directions.

We danced, we drank, we talked to that guy from the boat who liked to dress up like a cowboy. Kim and Jane talked with me for a while. It was a really nice party.

When Kris told me that it was almost time for the speeches, I decided it would probably be a good idea to excuse myself to the bathroom so I wasn't squirming in my seat during them. The ladies and gents were located outside the main function room, with both coming off a short hallway.

I did what I needed to do, and when I opened the door leading back into the hallway I almost ran straight into somebody. A chill went down my spine when I saw it was Daniel, who had walked straight past the men's room to wait near the door to the ladies'.

"Oh... excuse me," I said, trying to step to the side.

Daniel stepped into my path. "Hey, what's your hurry? I just wanted to apologize for the other day. I can see how that might have been out of line."

"OK... thank you. Apology accepted."

"There you go. See? We can get along just fine, you and I."

I took a step back. "What do you mean?"

He took a step forward, reaching inside his jacket to produce a wad of cash. "I've got a thousand bucks here."

My face screwed up and I tried to push past him again. "No thanks."

Daniel grabbed my upper arm and shoved me back. "What do you mean 'no thanks'? A person like *you* doesn't say no to a man like *me*."

I took another step away from him, but there weren't many left before the end of the hallway. My stomach started to churn.

"I-I'm still with Kris," I stammered.

"That's not what I heard. The way I hear it, your job is done. It's *my* turn, and since you're not a virgin anymore, a thousand dollars is actually pretty generous. Took long enough, that stubborn bastard almost lasted the week."

My back hit the wall. "He *told* you? Wait... what do you mean he 'almost lasted the week'?"

The smuggest look ever to grace a person's face crossed Daniel's. "You mean he didn't tell *you*? I was in on it from the start, remember? Kevin told me today, I thought Kris'd have the decency to fill you in after he... filled you in." Daniel laughed at his own joke.

"In on *what*?"

"It was all a big joke. We bet him double the cost of your pussy that he couldn't last the week without fucking you."

For the second time in as many confrontations with Daniel, I wanted to shrink down and scuttle away. The memory of that magic moment when Kris said he loved me seemed to shatter and start falling apart at the edges. My heart felt the same way.

"So, now you can come back to the real world. You're not going to get a million bucks every time you do your job. A thousand bucks is a real compliment, so take your money and let's go."

He tried to shove the wad of cash down the front of my dress, but I screamed and pushed his hand away.

"Feisty!" Daniel grabbed me by the arm, hard, and pulled me back towards the ladies' toilets. "Fuck now, pay later. Fine by me!"

He pushed my back against the door and it sprang open, but he never followed me in. A huge fist crashed into his cheek and Daniel stumbled sideways out of my line of view.

Kris flashed past the open door before it swung closed. I heard the sounds of a brief struggle outside and, when I peeked out, I saw Kris with one arm wrapped tight around Daniel's neck as he dragged him backwards towards the men's room.

Daniel's face was bright red, with blood pouring out of his nose, and his flailing arms seemed to be losing strength by the second before they disappeared through the door with the picture of a top hat on it. I tentatively stepped out into the hallway and braced myself with one hand against the opposite wall.

A woman I didn't recognize came through from the party, smiled, and said hello to me as she walked, oblivious, to the toilet. I may or may not have said hello back.

Kris emerged from the bathroom and rushed over to me. "Are you OK?"

I nodded, numb.

"Did he hurt you?"

I thought about how he had grabbed my arm, but it was nothing compared to what he'd said. I shook my head.

"I'll call the police," he said.

"No!"

Daniel was right. I was just a slut. Who was going to believe my version of the story, given why I was here? I'd be tying myself up in painful legal proceedings. Worse... what if it delayed my being able to collect my money and square everything away with the bank and save the farm?

No. I only had one choice. I had to get through tonight and tomorrow, then go home.

"No?"

"You stopped him before anything happened. Looks like I won, huh?"

"What... do you mean?"

"You couldn't last the week. You must have thought I was so fucking stupid."

"No! No, I didn't, Amy please. This is all a mistake."

"Hmmph. Whatever, let's get back to the party."

"But... well... I can get security to take care of Daniel... but we need to talk."

"We don't need to talk about shit."

"But you're..."

"I'm fucking *fine*. As good as a girl like *me* gets, anyway."

I stormed past him, through the door, and went back to my seat with my own personal thundercloud crackling away above my head.

# Chapter 25

# Kris

I tucked what looked like several hundred of Daniel's dollars into the front pocket of the security guy. If Daniel wanted it back when he woke up, he could fucking try it.

"There's a huge piece of shit on the floor in one of the stalls in the men's room. It's wearing a tux and looks like it's been in a fight. I need you to, discreetly, get it out of the building and put it in a taxi to anywhere."

"Right away, sir."

He signaled to his co-worker and headed towards the bathrooms while I raced back to our table. Amy was sitting in her seat, staring straight ahead at something a thousand yards past the far wall. I was no doctor but she looked like she might be in shock.

"Amy-"

"Don't"

"We need to talk about this."

"No. I'm fine. Please don't."

There was no way through her wall, especially when the music died down and Kevin took the stage to say a few words. I kept on trying until I heard my name and a light shone on me. I held still for a couple of seconds, but slowly rose to my feet and walked up on stage like a zombie.

Giving the worst speech since eighth grade, all I could see through the glare of the lights was Amy sitting all alone surrounded by people. She was hugging her own arms, squeezing herself down to something small and hard.

Eventually, Kevin rejoined me on stage and brought Anson with him. We all signed the document we'd agreed on and I only hoped I'd written down my own name correctly. Fireworks displayed on the screen behind me and the DJ played "Celebrate Good Times" over the speaker system.

Hands were shaken, many more got in my way as I tried to return to Amy. We didn't last long in the party after that. She stood up like a robot when I suggested we leave and stared out of the window the entire ride back.

Amy marched into her room, locking the door behind her while I paced back and forth outside, occasionally knocking and asking to talk. The speed at which everything had just turned to shit was making my head spin.

Just as I was about to knock on the door again, it flew open. She'd changed clothes, and I glanced down at her suitcase in her hand. Tears, ones she'd somehow managed to keep in check at the party, were flowing freely now.

"Amy *please*, I'm begging you, calm down."

"Calm *down*? You risked my home on a stupid *fucking* bet? Calm *down*?" she yelled.

"I never would have-"

"I might be just a piece of meat to you, but this was important to me. This was *important*, Kris." She dropped her suitcase and held her hands out in front of her like she was digging claws into a watermelon.

"I know it was. Let me make it up to you."

She shook her head. "How could I have let myself think you were something..."

"Something what?"

"Something... nothing," she said. "I have to go."

"You're *leaving*?"

Amy pursed her lips and looked like she might have been grinding her teeth too. She was on the verge of exploding.

"I don't want to stay here, but if you say you want to fuck me and I refuse during our week then by the terms and conditions of our arrangement, I default on the fee. A girl like *me* doesn't say no to a man like *you*, right?"

"Don't say that, Amy. I meant what I said today. I don't want it to be like that between us."

"What's it gonna be, Kris? Are you going to command me to fuck? Is that what you want?"

"No. I won't do that."

"Then I'm leaving. Goodbye." She grabbed the handle to her suitcase and headed for the door.

"Where are you going to be? I need to see you tomorrow."

"None of your business. You've got my number. If you want my body again before my flight, you can send me a message and tell me I have to come to work." Her suitcase rattled on the ground behind her as she walked out the door and headed for the elevator.

"Please tell me you'll talk with me tomorrow. This is something real between us, Amy," I called.

She slumped and I could see her face screw up as if something was trying to burst out of her mouth, but she didn't say anything. She stepped into the elevator and the doors slid shut behind her.

I retreated to my room, laid myself down on my bed and, for the first time in my life, I cried over a girl.

*****

If I thought I had bad sleep when I was trying to avoid Amy, that was nothing compared to how it felt when I thought I might never see her again. There was no response from her all night, and when I woke up with the sunrise after maybe an hour of nightmares, there was still no text from her.

I paced the penthouse for a while, sending messages and checking my phone the whole time. She'd worked her way into my heart without even trying, she simply belonged there. I never knew she existed before this week, and now the thought of never seeing her again was unbearable.

Around mid-morning, I had a flash of inspiration and went to my computer. I opened up all the major crowd-funding websites on different windows and searched through all of them. There couldn't be *that* many people trying to save a farm this way.

It didn't take long to find her listing. It was put up by "Amy E," the story matched what she'd told me, and it had a single donation of fifty bucks helping it on its way to the goal of three hundred thousand. Also included was a gallery of images showing the farm, wheat fields with some foothills in the background, a farmhouse, a tractor going through some other field. This was Amy's home.

I donated three hundred thousand dollars to the cause. Now no quirk of IFS terms and conditions could take her home away, yet I couldn't bring myself to command her back here. I needed her on her own free will.

She still wouldn't respond to any messages or answer her phone. After lunch, I went to the airport, several hours ahead of when I would have dropped her off today had things not gone to shit so spectacularly last night.

I paced back and forth in front of the huge check-in area until I could barely stand anymore, fooled every few minutes by a flash of blonde hair that never turned out to be Amy. Then I saw a woman walking towards the gate that said "Passengers Only Beyond This Point." It was her, she'd checked in already and I'd somehow missed her in the line. I ran to catch up to her.

"Amy!"

She spun around and my heart lifted when I saw the recognition in her eyes. There was no hate and anger there, but those windows into her soul quickly clouded over with sadness.

"Please don't go, Amy."

"I have to," she said. "Time's up."

"Fuck that. I'm so sorry for last night, for the bet, for everything. I wouldn't have done any of it if I had known you. But then, I wouldn't have met you in the first place. It was a fucked up way to meet, but don't let-"

She reached up and touched me on the cheek, tears welling up in her eyes. "I forgive you."

"Then...?"

Amy shook her head. "I have to go. I'm sorry. I was... foolish to open my heart up this week."

"But Amy... I love you."

"I love you too. But I can't be with you, not when I'm the girl you bought."

"You're more than that. You always were."

"Goodbye, Kris," she said, barely-contained sobs making her voice waver.

"Stay with me."

"I can't."

She rose up on the tips of her toes and gave me one last sweet, lingering kiss on the lips. I felt the tears on her cheek.

"Goodbye," she repeated, and walked out of my life.

# Chapter 26

# Amy

# August

I resettled the last new plant into its own pot and gave it a splash of water. When I returned from New Eastport, and after the celebration of our "miraculous" deliverance from the jaws of the bank, I set myself to work on my aloe vera inheritance.

It was a welcome distraction. I needed a lot of time to myself to think, and the aloe vera was nice and quiet. It never interrupted my train of thought.

We were out of the woods as far as our mortgage was concerned. We even had a bunch of money left over that my mom didn't know about yet. If I could make a business out of my plants and my story, the way Kris said I could, then my family would have a business that would provide for us for years to come too.

So I set about quantifying exactly how *much* aloe vera I had and reorganizing the haphazard shelving so it could grow and be stored as efficiently as possible. The toughest bit of understanding the state of my hopeful business was trying to figure out how fast the plants grew and how many new plants they generated in a given period of time.

I'd need to know that if I was going to have any idea how much I could sell. If I sold too little, I was missing out on sales. If I sold a little more, my total supply of plants would never increase. If I sold even *more*, then I'd be shrinking the size of my "plant factory." It was important to get this right.

In the corner of the greenhouse, my Bluetooth speaker played some music and I bobbed my head to the beat while squatting down to wash the potting mix off my hands using a hose. At the edge of my hearing, I swore I could hear a happy jingle like an ice cream truck playing under the sound of my music.

I tilted my head to try to hear it better as I turned off the squeaky tap that fed the hose. Drying my hands on my shirt, I pulled out my phone to pause the music coming from the speaker.

There was definitely ice-cream-truck music playing, but that was crazy talk. There was little point any trucks traversing our street, everybody lived too far apart here. Kids had miles of their own backyards to play in, they didn't gather on the streets. It made even less sense to come up each and every long driveway.

I popped my phone back into my pocket and picked up a rag to use to finish drying my hands as I stepped outside the greenhouse. Sure enough, there was a white truck with colorful writing on the side coming towards the farmhouse, kicking up a faint plume of dust behind it.

With a raised eyebrow, I wiped my hands on the rag and watched the truck pull up in front of the house. From this angle, I could read the writing on the side. In big swirly letters, it said "Creampie King."

The engine and music switched off and the driver exited on the opposite side. I heard a door sliding open on the truck, then shutting and he came out from behind his vehicle carrying some kind of small package.

I dropped my rag and held my hands to my mouth in shock when I realized it was Kris. Whether he caught the movement out of the corner of his eye or heard me gasp, his head turned in my direction. Our eyes locked.

He dropped whatever he was carrying and came closer... no, I was running towards *him* without even thinking about it. I only pulled my hands away from my face a split second before I leapt into the air and into his arms, wrapping my legs around his waist and my own arms around his neck.

I pulled my head back and kissed him on the lips, then buried my face against his neck, crying with happiness. He held me tight and rocked from side to side a little before eventually letting me slide to the ground again but never letting go.

"Kris... is this real?" I asked, looking up at him.

"I think so," he replied.

"How did you find me? Did Ada tell you?"

"Ada? No, she wouldn't say a thing. It's a long story. I guess... I hope... did you *want* to be found?"

I nodded, then wiped my eyes on his shirt. "I'm sorry! I... I was just so... overwhelmed. That night that Daniel almost... well... it was too much all at once. It took me weeks to wrap my head around everything, and then... I was too embarrassed to try to contact you. I thought you'd move on pretty easily."

"How could any sane man move on from you? I love you, Amy."

I smiled at him and, through the blur of my tears, saw the way he basked in it. "I love you too."

He kissed me again, his hands moving down past my hips to my legs, then back up again before wrapping around my back. I sighed when our lips parted and let him take some of my weight for a moment before getting my feet under me once more.

"What on *Earth* is this truck all about?" I read the logo on his shirt. "Creampie King?"

"Everybody I know thinks I've lost my mind. Who goes from tech startups to the dessert industry, right?"

"I was thinking, how many billionaire ice cream truck drivers are there?"

"Only one, but it was simply a means to an end. Finding you."

I offered him a confused smile. "What?"

"Well, you weren't on social media, the number I had for you turned out to be for a phone that belonged to Ada and she was no help, but I did have the pictures of your farm from the crowd-funding page. I knew you were somewhere in the corn-belt. So I started asking around, seeing if anybody recognized the area. All wheat fields look the same but those hills in the distance finally lit a candle in somebody's mind." Kris pointed at the Black Hills Range.

"But you can see those hills for..." I shrugged. "A *long* way."

"Yep. I needed an excuse to go door to door until I found you."

"That could have taken forever."

"Well, it only took a couple months. I would have kept on going as long as it took to find you, to ask you to give us another chance," he said.

"Aw."

"And, well, you remember you said I wouldn't be able to make a business out of creampies?" He gestured grandly at his truck. "You're looking at the fastest growing creampie business in the country. Believe me when I say, I've given a creampie to every man, woman and child in a fifty mile radius. For free."

Educated as I had been from my experience with InnocenceForSale.com, I was caught off-guard by laughter that would have been strong enough to make me cry if I hadn't already been doing so. My stomach hurt with it.

"And even a goat or two," he continued.

It was too much for me, I had to hold on to him to stay upright.

I wiped my eyes, the laughter trailing off into fits and starts. "That can't be a profitable way to run the business."

"It's not as bad as you might think. I include information for people to buy more off the website, and those orders are fulfilled from a distribution center. It runs at a mild profit now."

I shook my head. "It's no Annoying Creampie Jamming, but you just can't set a foot wrong in business, can you?"

"I set some feet wrong in other areas of my life though. I saw you refunded the money from your crowd-funding campaign. You didn't have to do that."

"It wasn't about the money, it never was, Kris. The farm was already saved. I didn't want money because you were feeling guilty. It didn't feel right. I had more than enough money left to…"

"To what? What have you been doing with yourself?" he asked.

"You inspired me."

It was his turn to look confused. "Inspired how?"

"To think big. Come have a look."

I grabbed his hand and led him in the direction of the greenhouse. Opening the door, I stepped in first and took him to the bench to spread out my drawings.

"What's this?"

"These are some ideas for packaging, for my aloe-vera-infused cosmetics line. Moisturizers, lip-stick, lip balms, all that kind of thing."

Kris flattened the papers one by one to look at them better, a little smile playing on his lips. "This is brilliant. You'll get all the benefits of your almost-free supply *and* your story, and the margins in this industry can be crazy. That's way better than pot plants at the farmers' market."

"I thought so too! I'm working with a co-packer to get the recipes finalized so I'll know how much aloe vera translates to how much of each kind of product. There's so much to do."

"This is really impressive, Amy. You're full of surprises."

"You're kind of surprising yourself."

"So, I was wondering…" he began.

"Yeah?"

"Can we put all the shit behind us? You never were just 'the girl that I bought,' but now you're *really* not. You want to go on a date with me? You know, just two equals, two small business owners with high hopes and more than a passing attraction for one another?"

"Yes! Of course!" I hugged him and inhaled the kind of cologne that probably no ice cream truck driver could afford. He hugged me back. "When?" I asked.

"Tonight. I'll need to get changed and offload the last of my creampies for the day. You know anybody in the area who would want a creampie?"

I smiled, holding back the chuckles. "Hmm, let me think. Well, there's Agnes Smith. She lives two farms down *that* way. She's in her seventies and I bet she hasn't had a good creampie in decades."

"OK, consider it done."

I cringed a little. "But my mom might be there too."

"Ooh, that's awkward."

# Chapter 27

# Kris

The last thing I wanted to do was leave Amy again after spending so much time finding her in the first place. However, with the knowledge that I was going to see her again in only a couple hours, I managed it.

She wanted time to figure out how best to explain "us" to her mom. When I delivered my last creampies of the day to this hilarious older lady named Agnes and saw Amy's mom there, I poured on the charm but didn't mention anything specific.

There was barely enough time to do everything I needed to do. I had to get back to Brenton, where I'd been living out of a hotel while going door to door in this part of the world and filling up my truck from a local distribution hub, and all the way back for a start. Plus, I had to rent a car since the only vehicle of my own out here was my truck.

Every door I'd knocked on in the last month or two was heart-attack-material. Always wondering if the next face I saw would be Amy's, wondering what her reaction would be if it *was* Amy.

When I finally *did* see her, it felt like my heart had been replaced by a bass drum that shook my body for a single beat. She was standing over by a greenhouse, hands covering her mouth in shock, such a sight for sore eyes that I forgot I was even carrying anything and dropped my samples and paperwork on the ground.

Then she ran to me. Once more, I had her in my arms, I felt her lips on mine and that perfect little body pressing against me. I could have held on to her forever.

It was strange to see her in this setting, this place she called home. I was so used to seeing her in expensive dresses, jewelry, her image perfectly manicured in the city lights, but it was still undeniably *her* under the dirty shirt and the ripped jeans, hair tied up to keep it out of the way.

Instead of flour on the tip of her nose she had potting mix, and I could have kissed it. If anything, she was even *more* beautiful now than I'd ever seen her.

If there was any question about how *much* of herself she'd shown me during our week together in New Eastport, it was answered when I knocked on her door that evening. She opened up and I saw that she had her heir tied in pigtails. Not high on her head like that unforgettable day in my penthouse, but long and flowing Pocahontas-style.

She knew what she was doing. If that wasn't a mischievous sparkle in her eye, then there was no such thing. Amy grabbed my hands with a smile that could melt an ice berg and sighed happily.

"You're here. Come in and say hi to my mom?"
"Sure, of course."

Amy pulled me in and led me to the living room. I saw the marks on the door frames Amy had told me about, I saw the way paths had been worn into the bare wood floors by years of her family's feet walking over it.

I'd never been in a house quite like it, certainly nothing I'd ever lived in felt like this. Even after only a few seconds I could see why she'd do anything to save it. This place was something special.

Her mom was sitting in the living room in her wheelchair, just as I'd seen over at her friend Agnes' house earlier. Her face lit up in recognition, another worry seemingly quelled. I had wondered if she would take issue with the large age gap between Amy and me, but apparently not.

"Kris, this is my mom. Mom… Kris," she said.

"Hello Miss…?"

"*Mrs.* Evans… call me Ellie."

"Well, nice to see you again, Ellie," I said.

Mrs. Evans' eyes dipped down to see Amy and I holding hands, and she almost visibly burst with a clucky kind of happiness. She clasped her own hands together in front of her.

"Ooohhhh! Agnes is going to be so jealous when I tell her my Amy is dating the creampie man!"

I may have looked like I was smiling politely, but if anybody paid me a closer inspection, they would have seen the way my jaw muscles were clenching my teeth together against the roar of laughter that was threatening to burst out. Amy covered her face with her free hand and shook her head.

"Mooooommm… don't call him that!"

Mrs. Evans held one hand to her chest and gasped a little. "Oh, I'm so *sorry*! I meant the Creampie *King*!"

It hurt. I wondered if I might crack a tooth from clenching so hard. Amy was holding her fist against her mouth, with little puffs of laughter snorting out.

"Amy, stop making such strange sounds in front of your friend, it's not ladylike."

"I'm sorry, Mom. Um. We're just gonna get going now."

"OK! Have fun! I'll see you out."

She rolled herself out to the porch behind us as I opened the passenger door for Amy. Maybe she'd been expecting me to show up in my truck instead of a high-end Mercedes.

"*Wow*! The whole state must be eating your creampies!" she exclaimed.

"Yes Ma'am, I'm the king," I saluted her as I circled over to the driver's side.

Mrs. Evans waved as we drove off and Amy was still shaking her head in disbelief until we reached the end of their driveway. Amy held my hand on her leg as we talked and I drove us to Stockville, a town about halfway between Brenton and her farm, for dinner.

After the meal, I never would have been able to tell anybody what I ate, because I couldn't remember. All I could see was this beautiful woman sitting opposite me.

In her face, I saw my own hunger reflected back at me. It was the kind of hunger that food couldn't touch. She looked like she wanted to do the exact same thing *I* wanted to do, leap over the table and fuck as hard as we could until enough police amassed to pull us apart.

We deserved the Nobel Peace Prize for resisting that urge until after the bill was paid.

"You should stay the night with me," I said, pressing my body against hers as she leaned back against the side of the car.

"OK, Daddy, but I guess I need to show you something first." She winked.

"Oh really, what's that?"

# Chapter 28

# Amy

The car ride and dinner were torture. All I wanted to do the whole way to Stockville was pull his hand up my skirt and make him touch me in the places only he and I ever had. Something told me, however, that it'd be all the sweeter if I could hold out for a little while.

The months since I'd seen him had been tough. The fantasies I'd been failing to suppress for a few years had all their restraints broken in my time with him. My imagination had been running wild on those quiet nights alone in my bed.

Memories of Kris' body, the way he felt inside me, the way he dominated his little girl, all vied for attention in my consciousness. Unfortunately, no memory could compete with the real thing.

Kris was like a switch that turned me on and set me free. The world sure as hell didn't feel right when I'd been humiliated at my old school, or when my boyfriend cheated on me, but I felt like *myself* for the first time when I met Kris. Then, when I came back from New Eastport and the farm was saved, a piece of me was missing.

It clicked back into place the moment I leapt into his arms. If "home" was more than merely a house or a location, then Kris was part of mine.

I was *aching* for the kind of release that only Kris could give me, and I knew exactly where we could go to act out a scenario that had built up in my mind ever since Anthony took me there. No doubt Anthony had been hoping to hit a home run with me that night, but I hadn't been ready. With Kris... I was born ready, and I knew he was as eager to play as I was.

Kris parked the car and switched off the engine. The hill looked out over the lights of Stockville and was quite pretty. The place was abandoned right now, because it was a school night, but it was a popular place for high school couples to come on the weekends.

"Why'd you bring me here, Daddy? This is where my friends all go with their boyfriends."

"You come here with your boyfriend?"

I looked away. "You know I don't have one. Nobody wants to bring me here."

Kris put one finger on my chin and turned my head to face him. "*I* brought you here."

"B-but why?"

"I've seen the way you've been looking at me, Amy."

"I... um... I'm not sure what you're talking about, Daddy."

"I see the way you're looking at me out of the corner of your eye when you're pretending to watch TV. I especially saw the way you were peeking through the crack in the bathroom door when I was having a shower."

"That wasn't me! I mean... it was an accident, I didn't know anybody was in there... I'm sorry!"

"Bullshit. Lately I've been making you so wet you can't think straight. Admit it."

"Daddy! You can't... you can't *say* things like that! I'm your daughter!"

"And you'll always be my little girl... but I know you want to be a woman," said Kris.

He unbuckled his seatbelt, leaned in, and I froze on the spot in mock fear. Kris played a *very* convincing daddy, and I was *living* my fantasy right now.

When he was close enough that I could feel the heat of him on my cheek, he paused. The scent of his cologne, with the undertones that were pure essence of Kris, wafted gently up my nose like some airborne aphrodisiac. I was just as wet as he'd said.

"I figure," he continued, "if you think you're ready to be a woman, I'm not gonna let some stupid fuckin' kid get his hands on you. You live in *my* house, you're *my* girl. *I'll* make you a woman."

"Like... kissing and stuff?" I asked.

"You've never been kissed?"

I shook my head. He was so close that even that slight movement almost made our lips touch. My heart was pounding, I couldn't have been more excited if I had been transferred to an alternate dimension where all this was *real*.

"Let's fix that."

Kris closed the last inch of distance between us and our lips touched. He started off gently, but quickly increased the forcefulness of his kiss until my head was pressed against the headrest and my mouth was wide open in the deepest kiss possible.

Our mouths parted with a wet smacking sound and I panted for breath. "Wow... Daddy... that makes me feel... um... so strange... good."

Still close, he leaned in and I felt his hot breath on my cheek, my neck, before he whispered in my ear. "That's your body getting you ready for a *big... hard... cock.*"

"Really?"

Kris kissed down my neck, across my upper chest and to the other side of my neck with those stubble-framed kisses that haunted my dreams and fantasies now. He grabbed my hip and pulled me in his direction a little as his lips tantalized my skin.

He was so big and strong, I could feel his power in the way he touched me. At any moment he could have ripped my neck out like a vampire or turned nasty, but he never would because he was my daddy.

"That feels *so* good," I breathed.

He moved his hand from my hip up the side of my body, lifting my shirt a little as it went. I arched my back when he cupped my breast, pushing myself against him, and smiled happily when he gave it a playful squeeze.

"Are you sure it's OK for you to touch me like this, Daddy?"

"No. It's not, but I'm going to do it anyway, because Daddy's little princess is the sexiest girl in town."

"We could get in trouble?"

"So much trouble if anybody found out how hard I'm going to fuck you."

"We'd have to keep it a secret?"

"Our little secret."

"Well... OK, Daddy."

His lips returned to mine and I unbuckled my seatbelt before letting my hands explore his body. The bulge of his biceps flexed as he pulled me close and then I caressed his broad chest as we kissed.

A moment of clarity hit me and I was almost so happy I could cry. His love for me, his white-hot *lust* for me, radiated out and I basked in it before slipping back into my wildest dreams again.

Kris pulled back and braced himself on the steering wheel and the back of his own seat, pulling his legs up from the area where the pedals were so he was kind of crouching on the seat. This wasn't a small car, but he was a really big guy and there wasn't a lot of room for whatever maneuver he was attempting here.

He stepped over the center console with his right leg, heading towards the back seat, and his ass hit the horn on the steering wheel. The lone luxury car on top of make-out-hill honked at Stockville below in the still night, and I giggled.

"I thought this was supposed to be a secret, Daddy? Do you want people to watch us?"

"Maybe some other time," he said, almost collapsing into the back seat before righting himself.

He reached through the gap between the seats to slide his arms under my thighs and behind my back, lifting me like I weighed little more than a feather. My transfer to the back seat was a lot more graceful than his, almost like I was a bride being carried over a threshold.

Kris set me down and lifted one of my legs to his other side so when he moved over top of me, he was between them, exactly where I wanted him to be. My body remembered him, and my legs wrapped around his waist, pulling the hard bulge of his cock against my wet panties.

"I've always known you were Daddy's little fucktoy waiting to happen." He reached down and cupped my sex through my panties, feeling how turned on he made me. "Look how fucking *wet* you are. You're so hot for me, aren't you?"

"Well… you *do* make me feel kinda funny…"

"I'm going to shove my big hard cock into that tight little pussy of yours, and even though you're so wet…it's gonna *hurt*. But… you're gonna like it anyway, you'll see, and when you do, I want you to say 'Fuck me Hard, Daddy.' You understand?"

"How much is it going to-"

Kris grabbed my throat and held my jaw between his finger and thumb. "You'll see soon enough. Now, when you like it, when you fucking *love* it… what are you going to say?"

I licked my lips and whispered in fake embarrassment. "F-fuck…"

"Yeah?" he prompted.

"Fuck m-me… *hard*, Daddy."

"Music to my ears, Princess."

Kris wrapped his arms around my shoulders and waist, holding me tight while he kissed me so hard that I thought I would faint. It was the kind of kiss that would definitely get a mention in the diary, even with everything else that was happening.

His hips ground his hard bulge against my panties, no doubt soaking the front of his pants, and sliding the silky material over my sex. After spending so many nights dreaming of the memory of him, my body ached to take him in, to make us one again.

Before pushing me to the point of unconsciousness, Kris released our lip lock and pushed himself up to reach up my skirt and grab my panties. I uncrossed my ankles and he tugged my underwear down.

His grinding had pushed the slick material between my folds and my labia held the crotch of my panties for a split second before springing out. The pristine white panties slid down my thighs, past my knees and Kris ducked under them when they reached my calves, leaving them strung out between my ankles with him between my legs again.

I couldn't help but imagine this place on a weekend, like the night Anthony brought me here, with the other cars around the hill parked and spread out as much as possible. How many times had the white panty-flag of surrender flown? Could they be seen through the windows from other cars?

Kris was bracing himself on one hand while reaching down between us. I heard the muffled sound of his zip and then shortly afterwards, saw him pull his cock out.

It had been all too long since I'd seen it, felt its intimidating presence, and marveled at how *big* it looked so close to my petite body. He pushed it down, so the shaft nuzzled against my sopping wet labia, and rubbed it back and forth.

My slippery juices coated the underside as my pussy lips caressed it. I felt the tip pushing at my entrance and held my breath, only for him to tease me by rubbing his shaft against me again.

The next time I felt the head of his cock pushing at me, the pressure only increased as it pushed my labia to each side. Once more, I was reacquainted with Kris' size, with the unavoidable self-doubt about my ability to take him inside me.

Yet, my body remembered this too. If I fought through the fear, if I pushed *back*, there was pleasure beyond belief to be had.

"Mmmnnnuh..." I grunted wordlessly in pain and effort.

"You're liking that big cock aren't you, little girl?"

I knew there was only one thing he wanted to hear, and one thing I wanted to say. "Fuck me *hard*, Daddy."

Kris smirked and pushed even harder. I felt a spike of pain, and then relief as my folds closed over the head of his cock and his shaft started sliding inside of me. Inch after inch filled me up until I was stretched to capacity along his entire length.

Now that he didn't need to use his hand to guide his cock into me, Kris leaned forward and wrapped his arm around my shoulders again. His lips were on my neck, then near my ear. I could hear him making little sounds that were the very essence of satisfaction as he moved inside me.

"Fuck... my girl's got the perfect pussy."

"Thank you, Daddy." I purred.

Kris' movements transitioned from incidental to full-fledged thrusts and his balls were soon slapping on my ass as he rocked the car from side to side. His hands were everywhere, as if exploring my body for the first time. He squeezed my ass, my breasts, caressed my skin, and held me tight, never relenting on those wonderfully powerful thrusts.

I moaned and yelped with every impact, feeling my breasts shake when he wasn't holding them and enjoying the rocking motion of the car. My panties were flung off my ankles by my shaking legs and the windows quickly fogged up so much that they were dripping.

The kind of fire that only Kris had ever lit between my legs was burning so bright that the line between pleasure and pain couldn't be seen because of the glare. I begged my daddy to fuck me hard, fuck me *good*, and he was up to the task.

With the magic spells that only he knew how to cast, pleasure won the battle and I felt myself building up to a glorious climax. My moans increased in volume with every breath I took and the pace of Kris' fucking did too. He pounded into me with more energy than one man should be able to possess.

I came. I almost *detonated*. A warm powerful humming sensation spread from my clit and throughout my body, making my muscles quiver and shake. A ringing built up in my ears, my breath caught in my throat, and I squeezed my eyes shut, cutting myself off from the world in every way except touch.

My pleasure and the huge cock pounding into my depths dominated my entire universe and then I felt Kris cumming inside me. I'd come off the pill after my week in New Eastport, my fertile depths were completely unprotected from his creamy seed.

The way his cock kept on twitching and spurting, it reminded me of that first time he came in my mouth in the photo-booth in Dreamzone, there was so much of it. I felt it leaking out around his ever-thrusting girth, making a mess of my skirt and who knew what else.

I wrapped my arms around his neck and held him close. His arms were around my shoulders and waist and he held me too. For time untold, we stayed like that. The only sounds were our panting breaths and the receding ringing in my ears.

I wanted to fall asleep like that, stretched tightly around his still-hard cock, exhausted and satisfied, held, loved, lusted after… everything was as it should be. I kissed him on the cheek.

"I love you, Daddy," I whispered.

Kris moved his head so he could whisper in my ear more easily. "I love everything about you, Amy. I love being with you, talking with you, fucking you, admiring you from afar and up close. I *need* you."

"I need you too," I squeezed him even tighter.

"I want to be with you. I can move out here, I can work from anywhere. Would you like that?"

"I'd love that, Kris."

# Chapter 29

# Amy

*Walking on Sunshine* started playing over my Bluetooth speaker and I skipped over to my phone to turn the song up. It was *exactly* how I was feeling. The music filled the greenhouse and I danced back to where I'd been working, picking aloe vera to send to the co-packer so they could make a test batch of moisturizer, the very first using my own plants.

The farm was saved, I had the opportunity to run my own business, and the missing piece of my life had arrived out of nowhere with a lifetime supply of creampies. I laughed to myself and bounced over to the wall to grab an old broom handle that was leaning against it.

My mom, who had been at my side for every humiliation life had thrown at me, didn't bat an eyelid at how much older than me Kris was. She knew, having had it explained to her in more detail than I could bear, what had gone on in my boyfriend's room that day a few years ago. She knew what I'd said and what I wanted back then.

When I returned from my all-night date with Kris, she welcomed me with open arms and a tell-me-all-about-it eagerness that I couldn't *fully* indulge. She said the heart wants what the heart wants and if I was happy than she was happy.

All she saw when Kris and I were next to each other was her Amy being adored in a way no guys my age had ever been smart enough to do. I had to hug her in relief when she said that. One day, soon, I'd figure out how to explain to her the full story behind how Kris and I met. A chance meeting with a seated creampie delivery technician was a good cover story though.

Kris was looking at property to buy in the area. He might even be able to pick up a neighboring farm and lease it out, like we were doing, while doing whatever work he needed to do from a home office or helicopter trips to the city as needed.

Using the broom handle as a pretend microphone stand, I belted out the chorus while striking a singing pose more than a little reminiscent of Elvis. Life was good.

The song suddenly cut out and I turned in the direction of the speaker, wondering what was going on. My heart sank and the broom handle clattered on the ground, dropped from numb hands.

Standing at the door, my phone in his hand, was Daniel. No longer hiding behind the disguise of an expensive suit, he now looked exactly like the kind of man he'd revealed himself to be that night at the Obvius.ly party.

With his unkempt facial hair, bloodshot eyes and dirty clothes, he was already frightening, but the way he was looking at me? Nightmare fuel.

Daniel put my phone back down on the bench and clapped sarcastically, with a sneer on his lips. "Bravo, you motherfuckin' whore. That wasn't the kind of performance I was expecting, but every cunt can get stars in her eyes once in a while, right?"

"What are you doing here?" I backed away a couple of steps.

Daniel matched my movements, keeping the distance between us the same. "You *owe* me. That cocksucker Kris owes me too. Did you think I'd just lie down and take it in the ass? Let him dilute my shares down before the sale so I got fucking nothing and just let it be? Oh *fuck* no."

"I don't know what you're talking about, but I don't owe you anything. You need to leave." I tried to sound tough, but couldn't stop myself from backing away again when he took another few slow ponderous steps in my direction.

"Oh, look at you. Did you take a fuckin' public speaking course after you retired from being a cum dumpster? Thought you'd hang up the ol' pussy and get into politics or something? You fucking worthless sack of shit. I'm getting paid."

My legs wanted to fold, to drop me to the ground so I could scramble under the shelves of aloe vera and hide, but I forced them to stay strong through sheer force of willpower. He made a sudden dash in my direction and I ran for all I was worth in the opposite direction, almost losing my balance as I turned the corner between two rows of shelves.

I heard an almighty crash behind me and felt a hot pit of rage ignite in my chest. He'd just smashed untold numbers of plants, my father's gift to me, and I wanted to turn back and beat him to a bloody pulp, but I knew if I did then it wouldn't go down like that.

Judging from the words spewing out of his mouth, the stumble had made him almost as angry as it had made me, as well as costing him some distance in his chase. I raced through the greenhouse, heading in the direction of the wall with the door, my heart pounding in my chest.

Skidding around the second corner, I saw that he was almost right on top of me, even with his misstep at the far end of the row. I screamed and arched my back barely dodging a swipe of his hand at my flailing shirt as he careened into more of my plants.

"You're gonna fuckin'..."

Daniel didn't finish his threat, instead opting to concentrate first on the capture. I saw my phone on the bench and prayed I'd be able to pick it up without slowing down on my way to the door.

If I could get my phone and make it to the house far enough ahead of him, I could lock the door behind me. Maybe I'd have enough time to call the police and find a weapon to defend my mom and me from this lunatic before he smashed his way in.

*Don't get ahead of yourself, Amy, you might die in this greenhouse yet...*

Sprinting at full speed, I flung a hand out and tried to snatch my phone off the bench. I almost cheered when I felt that familiar weight in my hand.

Cutting immediately to my left, I was only a few steps away from the open door when a hand shoved me roughly from behind, robbing me of my balance. I stumbled and flew head-first, reaching my hands out in front of me to brace my fall.

My left hand smashed through a pane of glass, cutting the skin from knuckles to forearm, an instant before my shoulder hit the frame, breaking the next pane up too, and showering my back with razor-sharp daggers of glass that cut straight through my shirt and stabbed me with fire. I would have screamed if the impact of my body hitting the ground hadn't knocked all the wind out of me.

Wheezing, dazed, I slowly turned on to my back and saw Daniel standing over me. Instinctively, I tried to shuffle away from him barely able to drag myself through all the broken glass and pain as I fought to breathe in some air, *any* air.

Daniel seemed to enjoy my struggle, seeing me cut and bleeding, struggling to breathe at his feet. He followed me slowly out the door, watching as each fiery breath into my lungs came a little deeper, a little easier.

Some invisible belt around my chest seemed to suddenly loosen, allowing me to suck in air normally again aside from the pain of the cuts on my back. I kicked out with everything I had, catching Daniel right on the kneecap.

His leg refused to snap, but he yelled out in pain, stumbling back a couple steps. It wasn't much. It wasn't enough. But it was all I had. I scrambled to my feet again and lurched to a run.

When my right hand swung in front of me I saw that my phone was, miraculously, still there. I didn't dare look behind me, didn't dare see how much my kick had slowed him down, because I wasn't exactly at top speed anymore either.

If I could just get inside, get to my mom. I could save us. I could save us…

My mom's wheelchair was on the front porch, but she wasn't in it. It sat uselessly on its side like a car wreck in a post-apocalyptic world, and my mom was nowhere to be seen.

I didn't even realize I'd slowed down until Daniel tackled me from behind at full speed, powering his shoulder into the middle of my back. My head whipped backwards, straining my neck enough to send lightning shooting down my arms painfully and my breath was knocked out of my body for the second time in less than a minute.

This time, when I hit the ground, Daniel's full weight landed on top of me. I swore I felt my bones grinding inside my body, but I still tried to look in the direction of the porch. What had he done to my mom?

# Chapter 30

# Amy

"What have you done to her?" I yelled.

I pulled at the ropes binding me to the chair, but I was no match for them. Now that I was secure again, Daniel broke his stony silence.

"I've got no use for that wrinkly old fuck."

"What have you *done* with her?"

"None of your fuckin' business. I didn't want that cripple bitch sitting around runnin' her mouth like you so I took care of it. You're lucky I've got a couple uses for that mouth of yours or you'd be fucking dead already. Now shut the fuck up while I make a phone call."

Daniel pulled my phone out of his pocket, tapped at it, and then cursed under his breath. He held the phone near my hand. "Unlock it."

"No."

*Crack!*

He slapped me so hard across the face that my head snapped to the side and my vision blurred for a second. Grabbing me by the jaw and digging his dirty fingernails in hard enough to make me whimper, he brought my head back to face him. I could barely hear him over the ringing in my ears.

"Unlock it."

I wanted to say no again, but my lips simply trembled instead. Daniel grabbed for my hand, but I bunched it up into a fist, making him spend a frustrating few seconds prying a finger out. Instead of pressing it against the fingerprint reader on my phone, it wrenched it backwards and I felt the snap in my finger as the bone broke.

I screamed wordlessly and felt a hot flush followed by cold sweat on my forehead as the pain radiated up my arm. Only then did he use my limp and broken finger to unlock my phone.

Ignoring me for the time being, he held up my phone and flicked through it for a while before holding it up to his ear. My head slumped down and I concentrated on trying to breathe through the pain.

How could this be happening? Fifteen minutes ago, I was walking on sunshine. Now, I was walking through hell.

I was in *love*, I had purpose and meaning in my life. Now, would I ever hear those three little words again? Would I ever say them again? Was my mom dead? *Dead?*

I couldn't bear to think about it, but a lifetime of thoughts stampeded their way through my mind anyway, all while Daniel held my phone to his ear. I never knew the *person* my dad was, just the idea of him, but I *knew* my mom. I knew her inside and out, and she knew me.

How does somebody like her change from a person to a memory? All the hugs and kisses, all the advice and understanding, the unconditional love... what was I supposed to *do* without that?

She spent my whole life in her wheelchair, which was now tipped over and empty on the porch, but she did the best she could to help me stand on my own two feet. For over two years, which stretched out to feel like forever, the ground under me had seemed so shaky until I fell into Kris' arms. Would we lose each other too?

I tried to concentrate on the most beautiful memories as they flashed through my head, to hold on to them and let them sweep me away. If things were about to get even uglier, I wanted my mind to be far, far away.

For a moment I was sitting on my mom's lap, laughing as she raced us along the paths in the park. The next moment, I was in Kris' arms, feeling his strength and the sense of calm after we made love. Then Daniel's voice cut through my reverie as he talked on my phone.

"Oh that's real sweet, but I don't think that was intended for me... Take one guess, you cocksucker... Right first try! Did you miss me?... Well now, *there's* a good question... Shut the fuck up... Shut the *fuck* up, you're not in charge here... Shut the fuck up and listen... Yes I've fuckin' got her and if you know what's good for you, and her, you'll do exactly what I say... You fucked with the wrong dude, Kris, you ride on my coattails your whole life and then fuck me over like that? Fuck you!... No fuck *you!* You can't even afford to pay me what I'm owed at this point, so I'm gonna be reasonable... shut the fuck up... The way I figure it, you need to bring me some cash and then I'm gonna disappear... Yes, really. I think two million three hundred and sixty thousand dollars sounds about right, don't you?... Yeah, motherfucker... I've got the bitch here at the farm, you bring it *in cash* within two hours and I'll be on my merry fucking way. If you're late... I'll have to start charging interest out of her pussy, and if you bring the police, well.. fuck it, she and I will go down in a hail of bullets with my cock in her ass... No... No, *fuck* you, you'll have to... Stole her *phone?* Are you fucking... Fine! Here..."

Daniel held the phone out to me. "Say something to loverboy."

I shook my head. Daniel snarled like an animal and grabbed my broken finger, twisting it. I screamed louder than I thought possible. White-hot molten *pain* exploded from my broken digit and threatened to melt my mind away completely.

"Speak, bitch!"

"Kris? I'm sorry... I love you..."

Daniel let go of my finger and brought my phone back to his ear while I slumped over, dribbling on to my shirt because of the pure agony emanating from my hand. Fresh tears flowed, fueled by guilt. I felt like a traitor, as if by speaking I was ensuring that Kris would get dragged into this, into being right where Daniel wanted him to be. I couldn't stand the pain, though.

*That's no excuse.*

Maybe not, but it was all I had.

*Keep fighting. It's not too late.*

I grit my teeth, trying to block out the pain, to find a spark of anger that could ignite a fire of strength. I couldn't, the pain and fear was too overwhelming. All I could feel under there was love. Love for my mom, love for Kris. It gave me the resolve to do what little I could to try to save him, even if it was too late for my mom.

*"Kris, call the police! Don't come-"* I screamed, before Daniel grabbed my finger again.

My sentence was cut off as anguished air tore through my throat, drowning out my words.

"Since when do you care what a bitch thinks, anyway, right?" Daniel said into the phone. "You just do what I told you, bring me the fucking cash within two hours. See you later, cunt."

Daniel hung up and then slipped my phone back in his pocket. He cracked his knuckles and then looked at me in a way that made me feel like I had slime all over my skin.

"You'll let us go when you get your money?" I asked?

His eyes widened for a moment as if he was taken by surprise, then he burst into laughter. "Oh, you poor naïve little bitch. Don't be stupid. He can bring however much money he can get his hands on within two hours, but I'm still going to fuck you and kill the both of you."

"No!"

Daniel stepped behind the chair I was tied to and reached down the front of my shirt to cup one breast. His touch was revolting, I tried to squirm away but there was nowhere to go. I tasted the acidic burn of bile at the back of my throat.

"Mmmm, we're going to have some fun alright, you and me," he said, "but first I'm going to get my money and kill him. That'll have to count as foreplay. I hope it makes you *real* wet or else this might be a fucking painful experience for you. Hey, I might let you cuddle up to his corpse while I fuck you, if you're into that shit. Hell, I might stuff a twenty into your mouth. I *know* you're into *that* shit, whore."

He pulled his hand out of my shirt and I gagged in revulsion.

"First, though, I've got a few things to do. Don't go anywhere."

# Chapter 31

# Kris

Every breath I took brought me closer to the Evans Farm, closer to Daniel and Amy. It also seemed to provide pure oxygen to a wildfire of seething rage that threatened to take over everything. I fought it down with everything I had because I needed to stay focused.

"Motherfucker!" I burst out as I turned into their driveway, and then clamped my mouth shut almost tight enough to crack teeth.

I couldn't even warn him not to hurt her, to give myself any excuse to let him live through the night. Yet, he could still hurt her *more*. That was why I had to get him away from her. Out into the open.

When the farmhouse came into view and my headlights washed across it I couldn't see any lights on inside, but there was an unfamiliar car parked just in front of it. Mrs. Evans' wheelchair was knocked over on the porch.

I gripped the wheel so tightly that my knuckles turned white. All I wanted was to feel those knuckles beating into Daniel's face, feeling it gradually get softer as his head turned into some bloody fucking mush.

He'd done something to a woman in a fucking wheelchair. How low was this son of a bitch, and how did I not see it long ago?

I parked the car and turned the engine off, but left the headlights on, pointing at the front door. The sky in the west was a deep orange, the twilight would soon be completely gone.

With a deep breath, I reached for the bag of money in the passenger seat and then stepped out of the car. I cast my eyes all around and didn't see any sign of anybody, but then a familiar voice came through the screen door of the house.

"Come on in, fucker. Hold your hands up so I can see them."

I held my hands up at either side, the bag of money in my left hand, and headed towards the house. It was only when I was at the top of the porch that I spotted any movement through the screen door. Daniel's head was peeking out at the edge of the door, but he moved away from it when he saw how close I was.

"Keep coming, nice and slow."

I reached for the door and opened it, stepping inside. My headlights illuminated the hallway and living room quite well. After taking a couple steps past the entrance, I could see Amy tied to a chair, with Daniel standing behind her, holding a gun to her head.

Amy had blood stains on the sleeve of her shirt, dirt all over the front, and she looked terrified. One finger of her right hand stuck out at an odd angle, and I fought anew to keep the rage down. He'd fucking pay for this.

"Amy, are you OK?"

"No." Her voice was croaky.

"OK, that's a real touching reunion, but you'll have plenty of time later to catch up. I must admit, I'm a little disappointed you're not late. I was getting used to the idea that I was going to fuck this whore in every hole."

"Well, I'm here. I've got your cash. Don't do anything even more stupid than you've already done, Daniel. I can let the money go. Nobody needs to know."

"He's-" Amy began, but Daniel pushed the muzzle of the gun against her temple.

"Throw the money over here."

Slowly and carefully, I threw the bag to the side of the seat Amy was tied to. Would he be distracted enough for me to sprint across the room while he bent down to pick it up and the gun was pointing away from Amy? I watched him intently, but he didn't even look at the bag yet.

"Take off the jacket. Empty your pockets," Daniel said.

I started shrugging my jacket off.

"*Slowly,*" he said, pushing the gun against Amy again.

I ground my teeth, but slowed my movements down, pulling the jacket off and holding it out to the side at arm's length before letting it drop to the floor. Next, out of my pockets came my wallet, phone and keys, which I let fall on top of my jacket.

"Hands up, all the way up, face the other way."

I did as he asked, finally hearing him move to pick up the money. *Fuck.*

"Is this all of it?" he asked.

"No."

"Are you trying to fucking play with me? *Now?* You *want* me to take the rest of it out on her ass?"

"Calm yourself down you stupid little fuck," I said, turning around. "I've got the rest of it. Here. In my car."

"Why d-"

"Because this isn't a movie where any sum of money you want can fit into a fucking little silver briefcase. There's over two million in the trunk of my car and it must weigh over five hundred fucking pounds. I had to scrape together whatever I could, there's even some fucking coins in there. Come on. Let's go outside, I'll load it into your car and you get the fuck out of here."

"You're not in charge, here, I am!" Daniel screamed. "I'm fuckin' done taking orders from you! You'd be fuckin' nothin' without me, you ungrateful cunt! Everybody back in New Eastport thought you'd lost your mind, but I followed you and I knew what you were doing. I knew if I was patient I'd get to pay you back for what you did."

"Fine, Supreme Leader Daniel, what do you want to do now?"

His face screwed up in frustration for a moment, then he growled. "Fine! Let's go, you load the money into my car."

"Great idea! Follow me. I mean, lead from behind, my lord."

"Shut your fuckin' mouth!"

I turned around again, keeping my hands up, and started walking away. After a couple of steps, I heard Daniel following and let myself bask in the wave of relief. Anything that got him away from Amy was good.

The headlights of my car made me squint my eyes when I passed through the front door again, but after going down the steps next to the wheelchair ramp I was soon out of their direct glare. Daniel was a few steps behind me as I rounded the back of my car and opened the trunk.

I glanced over at him and saw his eyes widen at the sight of so many bags of money as he peered in. The gun was pointing at my feet.

"Alright, start loading it up," he said.

"No."

"What the fuck do you mean "no"? Pick up the fuckin' money and load it into my car. You wanna die here?"

"A spineless little sack of shit like you doesn't have the balls to do anything to somebody like me. I'm not some old man in a wheelchair or some girl you outweigh by over a hundred pounds. You fucked with the wrong one here, I'm telling you that for free."

"Well, I'm the one with the gun, tough guy, so get to work."

"I don't work for you, motherfucker. Never have, never will. You've never had a good idea in your life, and this has got to be the worst. What was that shit you were talking about me riding on your fuckin' coattails? You delusional little fuck."

I could tell that every word that came out of my mouth that wasn't "yes sir" was pushing his fucking buttons. In fact, I was counting on it.

Yet, I'd have been lying if I said the world didn't slip into slow motion for me when his face contorted in rage and the gun in his hand started rising towards my head again. I swore I could see the glint of a bullet down the barrel and the way his teeth were biting his bottom lip as he was about to say "fuck you" to me for the last time.

*Bang!*

The shot made me flinch and brace myself for pain or death, and also brought the world back to regular speed. Daniel crumpled to the ground, blood pouring from his head.

The sharpshooter from the police had obviously judged the threat-level to be high enough to warrant it. I wondered if I'd cop any shit for pushing him over the edge instead of trying to talk him down. Still, like Daniel said, *he* was the one with the gun.

A scream came from inside the house, a scream like somebody's world was ending. I was on the move before the gun had even finished clattering out of Daniel's dead hand.

Racing inside, I burst through the screen door so fast I almost ripped it off its hinges. A moment later, I was at Amy's side, working on the ropes as she stared at me in astonishment.

Once untied, I pulled her on to my lap and she half fell into my arms, hugging me back as if trying to feel out whether I was real or not. I buried my face in her neck and hair.

"Where is he?" she asked.

"He's dead."

"I think he killed my mom," she sobbed.

"Did you see?"

"No."

"OK. We don't know that. We'll find her, I promise. Are you OK?" I asked.

"I don't know. Broken finger, maybe broken ribs. I don't know. I don't know. I don't know"

I put my arms around her shoulders and waist, away from potentially broken ribs, and held her even tighter. "Shhhh, it's OK. It's going to be OK. I love you, and everything's going to be OK."

"Love... you... too." Amy's words were staggered by sobs and winces of pain.

"Can you stand? Come on, let's get out of here."

By the time we made it to the door, the area in front of the farmhouse was bathed in red and blue flashing lights, and beginning to swarm with police officers. I led Amy in the direction of the approaching ambulance.

Before the closest police officer could reach us, Amy shook herself loose from my arms with a grunt of pain and ran back into the house. She ignored the officer's instructions to stop and, after a second of hesitation, so did I.

"Mom!" she screamed, bursting through the door again.

Amy darted from one room to the other, yelling and pausing to listen, until she opened the door to the closet in what must have been her mother's bedroom. She dropped to her knees and when I followed her into the room and saw around the door, I saw her mother on the floor in there.

Tied up, with a gag and a black eye but groggily moving and, most importantly, alive. Amy was desperately trying to untie her, but couldn't get a grip on the ropes through the blur of her tears and with her broken finger.

The police officer pulled out a knife and soon had her free, then ran off to call in the paramedics. Amy pulled her mother's upper body into her lap and rocked her, sobbing and stammering comforting words. I got down on the floor and did the same for Amy.

Minute by minute, as she calmed down, Amy's strength seemed to return. I could only marvel at her resilience. She was the love of my life, I was sure of it. Maybe from now on we could go for more than one week at a time without a disaster befalling us. Just a lifetime of peace wrapped in passion.

###

## Get FREE Downloads from Ada Scott

Thank you for purchasing this book! If you'd like to find out who is the surprise guest at the wedding of the century (for free!) then be sure to sign up for my **newsletter (http://adascott.com/free-bad-boy-romance-download/)** for a free and instant download of the story of Kris and Amy's special day. What they get up to *after* the wedding is HOT AS HELL and this extended epilogue is exclusive for Ada Scott subscribers.

Not only that, but there's also an exclusive short story about another one of the Innocence For Sale girls, Emma, who found herself in a pretty steamy situation!

As if all that wasn't enough, there are also exclusive extended epilogues available for each of Ada Scott's bestselling (as in they were all Amazon top 100 hits) Still a Bad Boy novels

I'm also on **Facebook** (https://www.facebook.com/adascottauthor) if you'd like to join me there.

###

**Enjoy This Free Chapter of Still a Bad Boy!**
# Chapter 1

# Kendall

I didn't dare move for fear of breaking something. If I did, I'd probably have to declare bankruptcy. It was only a waiting room, but I'd never seen such lavish attention to detail before.

If I wasn't mistaken, that was a real Van Achthoven painting on the wall. Even the receptionist's desk looked like something the President might have to save up for.

All glass, it seemed to be custom made to show off her long legs from all angles. She had them crossed, making her short skirt ride high as she tapped away on the keyboard in front of her, sometimes pressing the button on the wireless headset to answer calls.

Back home in Woodville I felt small. When I moved to the city, I felt tiny. Now, especially under her occasional disdainful glance, I felt positively microscopic.

I wrung my hands in my lap, second-guessing myself for the millionth time about the big move. I'd thought I'd show my family that I could be something, but I'd been here for months and I was still just an intern at *The Weekly Enquirer*.

My funds were evaporating fast. If my boss, Mr. Kinsley, didn't give me the actual job he'd promised me soon, I'd have to go home with my tail between my legs.

So why did he send me to interview Jace Barlow, the mysterious man who took his one hundred and eighty million dollar lottery winnings and quickly turned it into an empire pushing at a billion dollar valuation?

Was it because he liked my "moxie," as he liked to say to the people he actually paid to work? Because he saw some untapped potential in me? No.

As Mr. Kinsley said in the meeting room in front of everybody, as if I wasn't even there, Jace Barlow had scheduled and cancelled meetings with every major publication you could think of dozens of times. It was like a joke to the new multi-millionaire to screw with the media.

So send me to the appointment, and then when Barlow cancels again, at least nobody important will have wasted their time.

The receptionist's headset beeped and she pressed the button. "Yes sir? Of course, sir. Yes I'll tell her. One moment."

This was it. I looked over at the tall blonde as she unhooked the headset from her ear and stood up, smoothing her skirt. Was she going to escort me all the way to the elevator?

"Miss Brookes?" she asked.

"Yes?"

"Mr. Barlow will see you now."

I had to let that set in for a moment as my heart seemed to say "Right, I'm outta here" and tried to make good its escape via my throat. Swallowing hard, I managed to get it back down.

"What?"

"Mr. Barlow will see you. Now. You'll have to hand over your phone, and do you have any recording devices?"

I fumbled at my little handbag. "Uh... I've got a..." My mind went blank looking for the word. "Dictaphone!" I blurted out.

You could almost see the concentration in the receptionist's face as she tried not to roll her eyes at a so-called journalist who couldn't remember what a Dictaphone was. With shaking hands, I opened my handbag and took out the offending items.

The receptionist walked around her desk with a supermodel sashay and reached out for them. "I'll keep them in a secure container until your meeting is finished."

This couldn't be happening. A nobody like me doesn't interview the most elusive man in the city. Mr. Kinsley didn't even give me a questionnaire, he was that sure this was going to be a bust. I had nothing prepared to ask him and I was about to walk into an interview that famous journalists would kill their own mothers to conduct.

She confiscated the forbidden electronics and put them in a drawer before beckoning me through the door behind her desk. Once on the other side, I could see that the horizontal strips of mirror on the wall of frosted glass were actually one-way, so you could see into the waiting room like you were peeking out from a bunker without being seen.

There was no time to contemplate that though, as I was led at a brisk pace down a long hallway. At the end was a door, flanked by two men wearing suits and looking for all the world like Secret Service agents. One of them told me to hold my arms out to my sides as he waved a metal detector over me, while the other inspected my handbag for contraband.

I felt like it was a pretty thorough inspection before walking the plank. What would they do to me back at work when they heard I actually made it into Jace Barlow's office? I racked my brain trying to think of everything I'd heard about him, trying to come up with something halfway relevant to ask.

About a year before I would have been ready, the security men were apparently satisfied that I wasn't an assassin, and gave me the all clear. The receptionist knocked on the door and opened it, ushering me through before standing at my side.

If I thought the waiting room was expensively decorated, it had nothing on Jace Barlow's office. Everywhere I looked were sleek, sophisticated lines, fine furniture and tasteful art.

The man himself was sitting behind his desk, and my breath caught in my throat. I'd seen pictures of him before, of course, usually with a woman who looked like this receptionist on his arm. So I knew he was handsome, but I never could have expected what it would feel like to have those eyes on me in person.

All the luxurious surroundings and art in the world couldn't hide the fact that he wasn't born with a silver spoon in his mouth. I could see the edges of tattoos on his neck and arms, lurking just under the Armani, like snakes waiting to ambush unwary prey. He looked like if he flexed his muscles the suit would explode off of him as if he was a bomb.

Behind those dark eyes, I swore I could see thoughts beneath the surface that contrasted just as starkly with the cool exterior. None of the guys back home ever looked at me like that, and in this big city I was practically invisible. I almost felt naked in front of him.

It's a shame that the more you try to stop a blush, the worse it gets. I hated standing next to this beautiful tall woman. It was impossible not to notice the contrast between the two of us. She looked a lot like my sisters, and that was one of the comparisons I'd been desperate to get away from my whole life.

A barrel-chested man with a shaved head had been standing next to Barlow's desk, and now appeared to be leaving.

"Kendall Brookes, from *The Weekly Enquirer*, sir. Would you like coffee? Tea?" she asked me.

"No thank you," I squeaked.

She smiled and stepped out of the way of the man who was leaving, holding the door for him and following him out of the room. I heard the click behind me and gulped.

"Take a seat, Miss. Brookes," said the one and only, Jace Barlow.

###

**Check Out Ada Scott's Other Books,
including bestselling series Still a Bad Boy!
Still a Bad Boy (Still a Bad Boy #1)
Kendall**

He wasn't supposed to notice me. Jace Barlow: the most powerful man in the city. Mysterious, scarred, pure muscle and tattoos.

He was my first. That didn't stop him from pinning me against a wall, using me for his own pleasure until I screamed his name.

Now my boss thinks I'm getting the scoop of the century, but all Jace is giving me is climax after leg-quivering climax. When he puts his hand on my throat and growls in my ear...

"You are *mine*."

I know it's true.

I've fallen hard and I've never felt safer...

Until I see him kill somebody.

**Jace**

I dedicated my life to taking down the Picolli Crime Family from the inside. I made a name for myself, the mafia's most brutal enforcer. I worked my way up the chain, and my revenge came. A righteous bloodbath.

Then I took their place so they could never come back.

Nothing else has ever mattered. Until Kendall.

She was an innocent girl for me to defile, and then leave her *ruined* for other men like all the rest. But she makes me so hard I *ache* for release, and for the first time in my life, I want to have her again.

Kendall's the chink in my armor my enemies have been looking for.

I don't care.

She is *mine* and I'll die before I give her up.

### Submission Specialist (Still a Bad Boy #2): Skylar

I promised I'd save myself for my wedding night.

Of course, I *didn't* know it was going to be a fake marriage to a heavyweight MMA fighter. I *couldn't* have known how good it would feel to be pinned under all those muscles and tattoos, squirming, panting, and even whimpering in ecstasy.

*None* of us knew how deeply he was involved with the mafia.

When he disrespects them, they think they can use me to punish him.

They're wrong.

He's a tank in human form.

And he's coming for me.

**Austin**
Men tap out inside the ring, women surrender themselves outside of it. That's always been my specialty.

I chose Skylar because she was so innocent. A good girl like her would help sell my reformed image to the public. To corrupt her and leave her ruined for all other men would be my hottest conquest yet.

But I found more in Skylar than that. Who'd have thought that the first woman I wanted to lay more than once would be my wife?

Now they think they can take away what is *mine*?

Even if I have to kill every last member of the Bertolini Crime Family…

I'm coming for her.

**The F King (Still a Bad Boy #3)**
**Sarina**

I was always so focused on my career that I never had time for a relationship until it was my job to have one. I was supposed to "gain his trust," but I doubt they meant I should let him take me to bed.

Instead of showing me where he gets his supply of F,

he shows me what it's like to writhe in *ecstasy* as I scream his name. Instead of giving me the identity of the drug lord known as The F King, he gives me climax after climax.

My world now revolves around him so much that I can't tell which life is a lie anymore. I was an undercover cop. What am I now?

### Ryan

I thought Sarina might be a cop until I carried her into my bed and discovered she'd never been with a man before me. A cop wouldn't do that, and they damned sure wouldn't *beg* for more.

I wanted to destroy the Acardi Crime Family and build my own empire on the ruins. After all, I'm The F King, and a king needs a kingdom.

Sarina though… she makes me question my priorities. All that money and power is within my grasp, but the only thing I can think of is shaking Sarina one more time, *tasting* her, hearing my name on her lips.

If anything ever happened to her, to us, things might get really F'd

### Stockholm Syndromance (Still a Bad Boy #4)
### Eliana

My father kept me locked away from the world, my only purpose in life was to stand in the background while he campaigned for President, or to be sold like a slave to cement his old alliances as a Mafia hitman.

All I've ever known was his contempt and my loneliness.

Then my deepest darkest fantasy kicked my door down and dragged me off into the night.

He's the first person I ever met who wasn't afraid of my father. He's a machine of war, and he's making me *so... damn... hot.*

## Eric

The contract is simple: abduct the daughter of Jace Barlow's nemesis and deliver her safely.

I'm a professional. She's off limits... but this chick is the hottest kind of crazy. I never met a woman who could take everything I had to give and *beg* for more, and now I'm dangerously close to addicted.

I need to concentrate on keeping us alive before her father's goons, the Feds, the cops or the biker gang catch up with us, but the way she licks my gun has me thinking maybe nothing else matters if I can't have her wrapped around me *forever.*

###

71731696R00132

Made in the USA
Columbia, SC
05 June 2017